JAKE'S
DILEMMA

JAKE'S DILEMMA

MARVIN L. MILLER

bookhouse
PUBLISHING

bookhouse
PUBLISHING

2950 Newmarket St., Suite 101-358 | Bellingham, WA 98226
Ph: 206.226.3588 | www.bookhouserules.com

10 9 8 7 6 5 4 3 2 1

Printed in the United States of America

Library of Congress Control Number: 2021913695

ISBN: 978-1-952483-31-8 (Paperback)
ISBN: 978-1-952483-32-5 (eBook)

Cover design: Scott Book
Book design: Melissa Vail Coffman

To my wife Julie and my children,
Lisa, Mark, Jason, and Matthew

*"The record shows I took the blows
And did it my way"*

—Frank Sinatra

CHAPTER 1

Thursday, January 18, 1973
The Poodle Bar & Restaurant
Minneapolis, Minnesota

JAKE'S FIRST THREE NIGHTS MANAGING THE Poodle passed without incident. By ten p.m. on his fourth night, he decided that George the bartender's warnings of gloom and doom had been total bullshit. George was just trying to scare him.

Jake lit a cigarette and surveyed the half-empty room. He'd have very little to tell his ex-wife the next time they talked. A glance at his watch told him it was too late to duck into the tiny office at the back of the bar and restaurant to call Kelly and the kids; they would already be in bed.

"Mother fucking bitches, every one of you!"

Jake jumped at the loud voice that came from the end of the bar closest to the front door. A tall, muscular black man loomed over two girls in their twenties who were cowering on their barstools.

"A bunch of fuckin' teases, that's what you are," the guy yelled to the girls again.

Holy shit. This could get ugly.

He was halfway there when he saw George lean over the bar, his hands flat on the counter. "Hey, asshole." That got the guy's attention. George leaned even closer to him. "I'm going to fuckin' tell you like it is. You're leaving here the easy way or the hard way. It makes no fucking difference to me."

The man glanced back and forth between George and Jake,

probably deciding which of us to take on first, Jake thought with a gulp.

What the hell was he supposed to do here? This was his first test as the Poodle's new manager. He tensed and hesitated, then made up his mind. Clapping his hand on the man's shoulder, he tried to appear casual. "Come on. Let's go," he said.

The asshole glared at him out of bloodshot eyes, and Jake could smell the booze on his breath. He could also feel every eye in the place on him. This was no time to back down.

He grabbed the man's arm. Unfortunately, the man shoved him back. Jake nearly lost his footing.

George vaulted over the bar, and people to his left and right scattered. Jake had never seen anything like it—George's leap looked like something out of the comic books.

George firmly gripped the man's shoulder with both hands and nodded at Jake. "Grab his other arm."

Together, they forced the protesting man out the front door.

Outside in the cold night air, the guy broke away from Jake and took a swing at George, who ducked and hit him with a solid left hook. The man hit the icy sidewalk hard and stayed down.

Jake drew in a deep breath. His adrenaline was running high. He didn't know what to do. "What the fuck just happened here?"

Before George could reply, footsteps pounded on the pavement. Jake looked up and saw several men running toward them from the Hi Lo Club—what people from the suburbs referred to as downtown's "black bar"—on the corner. He counted eight men.

Holy shit. What had he gotten himself into? Eight against two. He hadn't signed up for this.

Nevertheless, excitement pumped through his body. His training in the Marines almost two decades ago kicked in. With his fists clenched and his arms up, he assumed a fighting stance. He was ready to go.

The men surrounded George and Jake, who instinctively stood back to back, facing the angry group.

Out of the corner of his eye, Jake noticed George pull a pistol from his back pocket.

"Okay, I'm going to kill six of you niggers, so who wants to be first?" George said calmly.

No one moved.

What the fuck? Someone do something! No! No one do anything! Still no one moved. Jake glanced left and right, watching the men silently decide what to do. A couple of them took a step closer to Jake and George, eyed the gun, then stepped back.

What was going to happen? What should he do? What did George expect him to do? Jake's mind raced. The guy closest to him caught his eye and sneered.

Jake stared, suddenly unafraid. Now the big question was who was going to blink first.

Brakes slammed in the street and everyone turned to look. Two uniformed policemen jumped out of a cop cruiser and dispersed the would-be attackers, as well as the crowd that had gathered. A couple of the men helped their buddy up from the sidewalk—the man who had started the whole thing. The cops gave a stern warning to the young men, ending with, "Get back where you belong."

Jake flinched when he heard the innuendo—fear had prevented George's earlier "nigger" comment from registering. Racism was alive and well in Minneapolis in 1973, but he was still shocked to hear it come out of a uniformed cop's mouth. No one else seemed taken aback by it though.

Also surprisingly, the cops didn't ask George about his pistol—if it was his, if he had a license for it—nothing.

Jake watched the black guys talking trash as they walked back up the street. The cops got in their car and slowly followed the group as they headed back to the Hi Lo Club. Jake turned to George, but he wasn't there. He'd already gone back inside the Poodle.

Jake couldn't believe what had just occurred. He sighed, relieved nobody had gotten killed, especially him.

As Jake opened the door and entered the bar, he noticed that he was sweating, even though it felt below zero outside. *Shit.* Was it obvious to anyone looking at him?

George was working behind the bar as if nothing had happened. His shirt wasn't even wrinkled, and the constant toothpick was still in his mouth, lodged in a corner between his teeth.

Jesus, Jake exhaled silently, then ran his tongue over too-dry lips. "Hey, George, can you pour me a tall glass of water?"

The toothpick bobbing up and down, George said, "Nah. Forget the water. What can I get you to drink?"

This was a surprise—an offer to drink on the job. *What the hell.* He could really use one right now.

"Jim Beam and soda," he answered. He waited as George poured it. Now that the danger was past, he feared he'd done very little to help. It was already weighing on him. When George handed him the drink, Jake took a big swallow and said apologetically, "I don't think I did enough out there."

"Are you kidding? The last manager would've been in his car and driving home by now."

If he had any brains, he'd have been in his car driving home by now too. That still didn't mean he'd pulled his own weight, but he nodded at George anyway.

George moved on down the bar to fill drink orders. Jake overheard him tell a few of the regulars, "That guy's gonna be all right." He jerked his head in Jake's direction. "I had him pegged all wrong when he showed up here on Monday."

Jake lit a cigarette, took a quick drag, and put his hands under the bar so no one could see that they were still shaking.

The rest of the evening passed without further incident. After closing time, he removed the till from the cash register and started toward the office, but noticed George sitting at the bar, looking hesitant.

"What's up?" Jake said. "Something on your mind, George?"

George put both hands flat on the bar and grimaced. "Listen, Jake. This is not easy for me to say, but I owe you an apology. When you started here on Monday, I kind of gave you a ration of shit because I really didn't think you were up to this job. You came in here wearing a suit and tie, and you'd never had any restaurant or bar management experience. I told Pat you wouldn't last a week. But the way you've handled yourself tonight tells me all I need to know." George pointed to his own heart. "You got it *here*, kid, where it counts, and there aren't many of us that do."

"Gee, George, if you get all mushy on me, I'm going to re-evaluate my opinion of you. I look at you and I see this six-foot, hundred-eighty-pound, ex-boxer with a crew cut from yesteryear, and I might start thinking you're a softie in disguise."

"Hey, don't fuckin' push it."

They shook hands and George said, "I'll see you tomorrow," as he left.

Jake locked up the Poodle, set the alarm, and walked to the parking lot, keeping a wary eye out. Once inside his '64 Mustang, he locked the doors and let it warm up in the bitter cold. It started easily this time; he usually held his breath when he turned the key in the ignition. The car already had more than a hundred thousand miles on it.

Jake put it in gear and drove out of the parking lot. He'd handled things just fine, now that he thought about it. He should have been scared shitless during that scene tonight outside the Poodle, but, instead, he'd felt strangely exhilarated—he still did. He pounded the steering wheel. "Goddammit. If that was a test, I aced it," he said as he smiled and pulled onto Highway 12, headed toward Wayzata. "It's going to be okay."

JAKE WOKE UP AT SEVEN-THIRTY THE next morning so he could call his ex-wife, Kelly, before she went to work and before the kids went to school. Even though they'd been divorced for more than a year, they still talked every few days, mostly about Sarah and Sean.

When she answered, he said, "Hi, it's me. I want to say hello to you and the kids. And do you have time for me to tell you about my new job and my schedule?"

"Okay. Talk to Sean and Sarah first," she said and went to get the kids on both phone extensions.

He asked the children how school was going and what they had learned this week. "And no one-word answers, please," he reminded them.

They eagerly complied and when they finished answering his questions, Sarah asked, "When are we going to see you, Fath?"

A warm feeling spread through him at the children's use of the nickname.

"Next weekend. We'll spend two whole days together and Saturday night, too, at my place."

After the kids were done, Kelly came back on. "How is it going?" Pleased that she was interested, he also knew she didn't have time to hear much. He'd have to keep it short and interesting.

"The head bartender, George Christenson, is a real character. He has this toothpick in his mouth at all times, no matter what he's doing." He told her about other people he'd met but purposely left out the incident from the night before, knowing it would upset her.

He continued, "The only negative thing about the job so far is that I have to work twelve nights on and two nights off, so I'll only be able to see the kids every other weekend."

"Oh, Jake, that's why the children looked so disappointed when they got off the phone with you. I guess that means you're not taking them this weekend. I wish you would have told me about this sooner."

"Why, does that screw up your plans?" As soon as the words were out, he regretted them.

"You know, Jake, being sarcastic and confrontational with me does not get you any points."

"I'm sorry. I keep putting my foot in my mouth when I talk to you, but I love you so much, and sometimes you act like you don't want to talk to me."

Much to his surprise, she ignored his remark. Instead she said, "Can you at least come over tomorrow early in the day, before you go to work? They miss you."

"How about you, do you miss me?"

Once again, she refused to take the bait. "So, Jake, what time can I tell the kids you'll be here?"

He sighed. "I'll be there at eleven o'clock." They hung up.

Pissed at himself for blowing yet another conversation with Kelly, he lit a cigarette and sat down at the kitchen table, frustrated. This thing with Kelly was getting worse instead of better—she hadn't invited him over to spend the night for weeks.

He needed some advice—or maybe he just needed to vent. He picked up the phone again and called his longtime friend, Marshall

Ferster. Marshall knew Kelly pretty well; the two couples had been over at each other's houses often enough when he and Kelly were still married.

He caught Marshall before he left for work. "Marshall, it's Jake. Got a minute?"

"Jake, hey, good to hear from you. How's that new job going? What's the name of that guy you're working for?"

"The owner of the Poodle is Pat Blumenthal. He seems like a good guy so far, but that's not really why I called." He ground out his cigarette and reached into the pack for a new one, lit it, and took a deep breath. "I just can't seem to say the right thing when I talk to Kelly. I put my foot in my mouth, and I get all territorial. I still love her more than ever, and I want to get back together."

"Well, Jake, as your friend, I can say this: Maybe when you were married, if you'd been less of an oink-oinker, you wouldn't be in this situation. Have you changed all that much, and does Kelly realize this?"

"Sure, I have," he said quickly. "I didn't realize how much I loved her then, but now I do."

"Listen, Jake, if you're asking me for advice, I can't give you any, except to say that, sometimes, when it's over, it's over."

"Gee, I sure am glad I called you." He slammed down the phone. Well, that had really made him feel better.

GEORGE GREETED JAKE THAT EVENING AS if they were old friends. Just as Jake thought—last night had been his rite of passage.

George asked him, "Is Jim Beam and soda your preferred drink?"

Jake replied in the affirmative and George poured him one. "This one's on Pat," he winked. "But he won't know it."

This is pretty cool, he decided. A drink every now and then would help keep him relaxed, especially if they had more incidents like they had last night.

Jake leaned against the bar and sipped his Beam and soda while George gave him a rundown of the bar patrons. The inside scoop, so to speak. "See, over there is Jimmy Box. The fucker's a stone-cold killer. Last year, he allegedly shot a man in the back and got off with self-defense."

"No kidding? I bet his lawyer was Ron Meshbesher." Jake added, "I went to school with his younger brother, Kenny."

"Right you are," George nodded. "Meshbesher got him off. So, when you talk to Jimmy, show him a little respect because you really don't want to get on his bad side. But if we ever have any trouble in here that requires more muscle, we can count on him."

He continued down the list, pointing out people around the room. "Okay, sitting next to Jimmy is The Polack—the big ape is not to be trusted!"

"Why? What's his story?"

George shrugged. "He's just a burglar. Been in and out of the slammer. And, between you and me, he's a fuckin' snitch. And here's another tip: Any time you get two crooks talking to each other, walk away, because they'll soon be talking about some job one of them just pulled. They're all snitches. They'll drop a dime on each other in an instant. You don't want to be caught in the middle of that."

He pulled the tap on Hamm's beer and passed a frothy glass of it to someone who'd just walked in and slid onto a barstool. The customer nodded his appreciation.

George said in an undertone to Jake, "Oh, and I almost forgot to mention some other fuckers that are not here at the moment. Two real bad assholes: Dutch Lundgren, and maybe the biggest and most dangerous prick of all, Lucky Doyle. I'll point them out to you when they come in."

Great, Jake thought. He'd be sure to avoid them. Forewarned was forearmed.

George continued around the room, pointing out the type of people who frequented the Poodle. "Lots of cops come in." He glanced at Jake and grinned. "I see the surprised look on your face. The cops love this fuckin' place because they know where to find the bad guys."

George looked like he was done talking, so Jake asked a question that had been on his mind. "Who's that funny little guy who sweeps the floor around here? What's his story?"

"That's Leonard Kazinski. Lenny comes in a few hours a week

to sweep and do other odd jobs. He makes most of his money off what he finds on the floor; some of the customers drop coins just so Lenny will pick them up. He can't read or write—just signs his name with an X. But don't underestimate him. If you ever need help with someone, you just tell Lenny to grab the guy. His arms are like fuckin' vices—once he gets a grip, there's no escape."

"Well, he really is an odd duck. I've talked to him a few times and he keeps calling me Mr. Jake, despite me telling him to drop the Mister. I guess I'll throw him some coins now and then too."

The Poodle catered to the downtown business crowd at lunchtime, but from what he'd seen so far, the crowd at night was a lot rougher around the edges. Mostly crooks, wannabe crooks, cops, hookers, a few average Joes, and people slumming who wanted to see how the other half lived.

He shook his head at the dichotomy in the customer base. Just his luck to get stuck on the night shift. He'd have to take charge and show this crowd that he was the boss. And he'd have to figure out a way to control them when incidents occurred again like the one last night.

The best way would be to treat them all the same, he decided, and show no preferences. He'd learned this when he managed a plumbing company; it appealed to his sense of order and fairness.

"Oh, by the way," George said, drawing Jake's attention. He reached into his back pocket and pulled out a blackjack. "Here, take this. I'll get another one from my cop buddies."

Jake took the five-inch leather strap. The weapon was weighted on one end. He thumped it in his hand to get a feel for it. "Gee, George, I've only seen these in the movies, but thanks." He slapped it a few more times, then stuck it in his right back pocket.

All night long, he was aware of the bulge in his pocket. Confidence filled him. He now had a weapon *and* George's trust that Jake would get the job done if some unruly bastard got out of hand.

As the evening ended, George said to Jake, "Hey, I'm going over to Jimmy's Broiler across the street for some breakfast. Why don't you join me?"

Jake nodded at George and grinned. The invitation confirmed that Jake was now one of the boys.

CHAPTER 2

Monday, January 22

JAKE'S SECOND CHALLENGE occurred on Monday night. About nine o'clock, an unruly customer caught his attention. The guy was mouthing off and giving George a ration of shit because he wouldn't serve him another drink. Already unsteady on his feet, the man was swearing a blue streak.

As Jake hustled over, George gestured with his head. "Jake, get this mother fucker outta here before I deck him."

He could do this! Jake opened his arms wide and grinned confidently. "No problem! I'll take it from here."

He instinctively felt in his back pocket to verify the blackjack was there. Yes, he had this one.

Jake grabbed the guy's arm, then pushed and followed him out the door. In the icy night air, the man flung off Jake's grip. The guy swung around to face Jake, his fists clenched and coming up in a fighting position. Jake swallowed hard, suddenly realizing that this asshole was considerably bigger and heavier than he was.

Oh, fuck. Jake began to do the same thing but decided the blackjack would be more effective than anything his fists could do. He whipped it out and whacked the guy on the side of the head.

Nothing happened.

He had to put more into this one. Jake swung again, as hard as he could.

Nothing happened.

The guy shook his head a couple times as if to clear it, and grunted, then muttered something Jake couldn't understand. Jake shivered in the freezing temperature. The streetlights illuminated the sidewalk enough that Jake could see the man blink, then narrow his gaze and glare at Jake.

Jake's first thought was to run, but he ruled that out because he'd appear gutless. He'd rather face this asshole than have people in the Poodle think he was chicken shit.

But now what the fuck was he supposed to do? He glared back at the man, hoping to stare him down.

It must have worked because the guy blinked again, then turned and, cursing to himself, staggered away.

Jake took a couple of deep breaths, looked up, and said, "Thank you, God." He heaved a sigh of relief, then shivered. It was damn cold out here.

He walked back in the bar and gave George the thumbs-up sign. George nodded and went back to serving drinks.

Jake looked at the blackjack still in his hand. He obviously needed something bigger than this. He strode to the office to look around. He searched all of the desk and file cabinet drawers and finally found a big fourteen-inch club with an attached leather string to wrap around his wrist, which he did. He smacked the club against the palm of his hand. "Ouch!" he yelped, then grinned. "This ought to do the trick."

He locked the office behind him and showed the club to George, who raised his eyebrows. "You're going to fuckin' kill somebody with that."

Jake laughed. "And your point is?"

AFTER CLOSING, JAKE AND GEORGE WENT across the street to Jimmy's Broiler for breakfast again. Open twenty-four hours a day, it was one of the places most frequented by those in the restaurant and bar business, George explained.

"Jake, I'm going to give you some advice on how to survive in our home away from home. First and most important," George paused, "well, let's face it, you're not very big. What are you, about five-ten, a little less than one-seventy?" Jake nodded warily. George continued, "So make sure you hit them first, hit them last, and never let them get the fuck up! If they do, you're in big trouble."

What was he? Chopped liver? Jake opened his mouth to respond, but George held up his hand.

"I'm not finished. Next thing is you have to stay in shape. I run every morning on railroad tracks with heavy boots. This builds up my stamina, so I can go a few rounds if I have to. The reality is that ninety-five percent of the guys don't want to fight, and of the five percent that do, most of them don't know how. And those that do, well, they can't keep their arms up swinging for more than a couple of minutes."

Jake had done some boxing in the Marine Corps, but George was on a roll so he didn't interrupt to mention it.

"Here's another tip. When you're facing a potential problem, watch his eyes and his hands. They tell you all you need to know. If he's shouting at you, that's better than those who don't say anything. The quiet ones are the ones to be concerned about."

Jake nodded. That was a good tip.

George leaned back in his chair. "Oh, and another thing. If you want to have a few drinks, Jake, that's okay, as long as it doesn't interfere with the job."

Jake nodded again. A thought occurred to him. "George, how come I never see you take a drink?"

George laughed. "I was an alcoholic for years. I used to get falling down drunk at the bars. Some fuckers would try to pick a fight with me and I would say, 'maybe you will beat me tonight but I will be sober and at your front door tomorrow morning with a fuckin' baseball bat.'"

Jake leaned forward, interested. "So, how did you quit drinking? Join AA?"

"Nah, I just decided one day and that was it. I haven't had a drink in three years and don't miss it."

"Wow, that's heavy." Quitting alcohol cold turkey was a sign of a strong character.

The waitress brought their order. Jake dug into his bacon, eggs, and toast—his favorite meal. Halfway through clearing his plate, Jake asked a question that had been on his mind.

"I know that Pat's the owner, but what's the deal with Pat's old man and the ugly broad that hangs around with him? They're both in a lot."

George took a sip of coffee before answering. "The first thing you need to know is that Pat and his father, Carl, are fifty-fifty owners. And the broad, who we not so affectionately call the Dragon Lady— she can be a real pain in the ass. She doesn't fuck with me because I would rip her a new one and she knows that. But just remember that she watches the place and is a snitch. The good thing is she typically goes home around ten o'clock on the nights she's here."

Oh, this was great. He had more than one boss, and a snitch looking over his shoulder. He thought about the ramifications of this news. "So I probably shouldn't have a drink in front of them?"

"Suit yourself," George shrugged, "but it's probably a good idea to wait until they leave."

Now Jake was the one on a roll. "George, do you have a main squeeze?"

"Yeah, her name's Joyce and she's a waitress over at the Blue Ox. We've been going together about a year. How about you?"

Jake hesitated, then decided. *What the hell.* "Married for ten years, divorced now. Got two great kids, ten and eight. They live with their mom over in St. Paul."

"I suppose, like most exes, she's always busting your balls, right?" George grinned sympathetically.

"No, it's nothing like that. We've been divorced for a little over a year, and it's kind of an on-and-off relationship. More off than on," he lamented.

"Well, if you ever need pussy, there are plenty of broads that come into the Poodle that are worth fucking. You shouldn't have any trouble."

DESPITE A CONFRONTATION ALMOST NIGHTLY, THE days flew by. He missed Kelly—missed coming home to her at night, hearing about her day. He wished he could tell her how wild and crazy the Poodle really was, but he didn't want to worry her. She had enough on her plate, being a single mom. "And whose fault is that?" a little voice in his head asked him.

One afternoon in late January, Jake noticed that while driving to work—in below-zero weather, no less—his armpits were wet before he even got there. Obviously, the anticipation of what would happen each night was getting to him.

What the hell was he doing, working at the Poodle? How much over his head was he? He pulled his Mustang into a parking spot in the lot where he and the other Poodle employees parked. He let the car idle. Here I sit, he thought, analyzing why I have wet armpits, when I should be getting my head examined. What's a nice Jewish boy from north Minneapolis doing in a situation like this?

He shook his head and shut off the car. What was that old saying? *I'm a lover, not a fighter.* No wonder he was a mess.

He had already gotten in the habit of fortifying himself with a couple belts as soon as Pat went home. When that proved not to be enough, he had added a third. And sometimes a fourth. Hell, if he was going to be at risk of physical injury every day, he could damn well drink as much as he wanted.

He had tested the waters by having one or two of those drinks before the old man and the dragon lady went home. When he didn't get any feedback, he felt more confident drinking his liquid courage in front of them, so it was no longer a concern.

Jake picked his way along the icy sidewalk. At the door to the Poodle, he straightened his tie, lit a cigarette, and walked inside, quickly scanning the room to see who was there. By now, he knew most of the regulars by name, and their quirky habits too.

Harry Gruber came in every evening after he got off work, about five-thirty, and sat at the far end of the bar, closest to the dining room. He had four or five drinks, never caused a problem, and was friendly enough. He didn't order dinner, but he liked his brandy and soda. Like most of the regulars, he was a creature of habit.

Tonight, though, Harry was standing near the bar, his hands on his hips. As soon as he saw Jake, he strode over and got in his face. "Somebody's sitting on my stool!"

Jake reared back. "What the fuck are you talking about, Harry? Just sit somewhere else."

"You don't understand. *That's. My. Stool!*" he said, punctuating each word by stabbing his finger at the occupied stool.

Jake rolled his eyes, went over to the guy sitting there, and asked him to move over one.

The man looked like he thought Jake was crazy, but he reluctantly slid over to the next seat.

"You happy now, Harry?"

He nodded. "Just remember, that's my spot."

Jake said to George, "Buy Harry a drink on us." That seemed to pacify Harry, who had quietly taken his seat.

Jake just shook his head.

The next day, Jake related the story to Pat, who said, "You gotta understand something. This place is like a country club to some people."

"How's that?" *Has Pat looked around this shithole lately?*

"People go into a country club to sit around, drink, and seek companionship. It's like a home away from home. That's what this bar is for some people—a home away from home."

Jake just shook his head. Likening the Poodle to a country club was bizarre. It sure as hell wouldn't have been his first choice. Or his second. He shrugged. Well, you learn something new every day, he thought.

BY FRIDAY EVENING, JAKE WAS LOOKING forward to his two days off—Saturday and Sunday—and spending time with his children. He called Kelly. "What time should I pick up the kids tomorrow?"

Much to his surprise, she responded, "Why don't you come over tonight after work, so you can be here when the kids wake up in the morning?"

Jake agreed and hung up the phone. He smiled heavenward. "Yes! Thank you, God. I might get lucky tonight!"

CHAPTER 3

Saturday, January 27

KELLY ROLLED OVER and gently poked Jake. "Are you awake?"

"Why, are you interested in trying for a third time?"

She laughed. "Quit dreaming. You were pressed when it came time for seconds. Go shower and get dressed before the kids wake up."

Jake kissed her and reluctantly got up. In the shower, he wondered why it couldn't have been like this when they were married. Maybe, just maybe, they could get back together if he got his act straightened out.

He turned off the water and grabbed a towel. Nah, they tried that once before and it hadn't worked. "But, it doesn't mean we can't continue to try," he argued with himself.

He went back into the bedroom to get dressed. Kelly was slipping into a pair of jeans and watched him step into his shorts.

"Jake, you have two things going for you. You have that full head of wavy brown hair, and great legs. When they go, you'll be in big trouble, but for now, you're a good-looking man . . . except for that silly mustache. When are you going to get rid of it?" she asked him.

"Well, if you remember, my dear, I grew the mustache and a beard last summer, after we got divorced and I went through my period of mourning." He grinned at her. "But I decided I would have to cut them off because they were inappropriate for selling insurance. The kids saw me shaving and begged me not to. I compromised by shaving off everything except the mustache. That seemed to pacify them."

"Hmm. Well, it tickles."

"Get used to it. The kids want it; I'm keeping it," he shrugged. That was the end of it as far as he was concerned.

After getting dressed, he went downstairs, put a load of laundry in the washer, and made breakfast. Bacon and pancakes, the children's favorite. Goddammit, he missed these special moments with the family. When they were married, he hadn't done anything to help out. Now he realized the error of his ways, but was it too little too late? He hoped to hell it wasn't.

He could hear Kelly waking up the kids, and soon they came bounding down the stairs. Sarah, at ten, and Sean, at eight, were both bright and loving children. Sarah, with dark-brown hair, looked more like Jake, and Sean had the same blue eyes and auburn hair as Kelly.

They wrapped their arms around him while he flipped pancakes.

"I love you, Fath," Sarah said.

"Me too," Sean added.

He gave them both a hug and showed them his trick for flipping pancakes. "It's all in the wrist."

He tried to spend as much time with them as he could, but it was never enough. How much the divorce affected them, he wouldn't fully know until years later. He felt guilty that Kelly had to go to work now; she'd stayed home—happily, he thought—when they were married. Now Sarah and Sean were latchkey kids. He shrugged off his melancholy.

The kids asked him to take them ice skating at the rink in St. Paul. Jake agreed reluctantly because he couldn't skate worth a shit, but if it's what they wanted, he would do it. Kelly had to work, so after she hugged them all good-bye, he bundled the kids in his car and set out.

AFTER A DELIGHTFUL WEEKEND WITH THE kids and Kelly in St. Paul, he drove home to Wayzata on Monday morning to get cleaned up before he headed to work.

Jake lived in the old section of this Minneapolis suburb, where he rented and shared a nondescript rambler with Pete Olson. He and Pete were both divorced. They generally got along, but Jake's biggest complaint was that Pete drank too much. He couldn't complain about the rent, though, since Pete was only charging Jake a hundred a month.

Jake had his own room and bathroom. He and Pete occasionally brought women home, which worked out okay since their bedrooms were on opposite ends of the house. When the kids slept over, Jake unrolled sleeping bags on the floor of his room and they pretended they were camping.

Jake's longtime friend, attorney Neal Phillips—commonly known as the Judge although no one remembered why—stopped in at the Poodle a couple times a week. Not just because of Jake, but because he picked up clients from time to time in the various bars on Hennepin Avenue, where the Poodle was located. The Judge had also done some work for Pat last December, and it had come up in conversation that he was looking for a nighttime manager. The Judge had recommended Jake. When Jake took the job, he thought it would involve more management duties, but now that he'd been here a few weeks, he realized he was just a glorified bouncer.

One night in early February, Jake came out of the office and noticed the Judge sitting at the bar, pontificating to anyone who would listen. Jake liked the Judge; however, if the truth be known, he felt that Neal wasn't much different from an ambulance chaser. He'd never told the Judge that, of course.

At just over six feet and about 230 pounds, Neal looked like a big teddy bear. His preferred drink was a VO and soda. Jake ordered one for him on the house.

Since Jake wasn't busy and he still had some questions about the owner's father, Carl Blumenthal, he decided this would be an opportunity to get answers. Knowledge was power, Jake believed. Jake asked the Judge, "So what's the story with Blumenthal's father? He and the Dragon Lady can be a real pain."

Neal left his stool at the bar and indicated for Jake to follow him to one of the tables in the back. "I don't like to compete with the noise, and some of what I'm going to tell you is not for public consumption," the Judge said quietly, casually looking around to see who was nearby.

Jake smiled to himself. The inside scoop—excellent. He sat down and hailed the waitress.

"Same as before?" she asked. The two men nodded and Jake said to her, "Just keep the drinks coming and don't bother me unless it's really important."

According to the Judge, Carl was born in Romania in 1902 and came with his family to America when he was four. They settled in Pittsburgh and after two years, they moved to Minneapolis because they had relatives there. Carl went to North High and the Northwest College of Chiropractic—

Jake interrupted, "No shit? He's given me a neck adjustment on a few occasions; no wonder he's so good at it."

The Judge nodded. "He practiced five or six years, but his older brother, a medical doctor, was embarrassed to have a chiropractor in the family and urged Carl to find another livelihood."

The Judge was quiet for a moment, and Jake grew irritated with the waitress because she still hadn't brought their next round. He stood up to go find her. He and Neal shouldn't have to wait this long. She saw him immediately and mouthed, "I'll be right there." A minute later, she hustled over and deposited the men's drinks.

Jake sat back down and the Judge continued. "Anyway, so Carl bought a grocery store. Then he bought a beer joint in Robbinsdale. After he sold that, he bought the 114 Club on Washington Avenue. The rumor is that he was running numbers out of the place and using booze that came from illegal stills, and he charged an obscene amount to cash people's checks."

Holy shit, what kind of people was he working for? Jake shifted uneasily in his chair.

"Finally, he bought the Poodle in 1960." The Judge sat back in his seat and toyed with his now empty glass.

Jake got the hint and signaled to the waitress to bring another round. "Keep talking," he told the Judge. "I love to hear this stuff." You just never know when this information will come in handy, he thought.

The Judge continued, "Pat worked at the Poodle from the start, but he had an older brother working here as well."

"Wait a minute, this is the first I heard about a brother here. What happened? Where is he?" Holy fuck, there was another Blumenthal running around?

The Judge leaned forward and, in a lower voice, explained, "His name was Sid. Tall and good looking. A real ass man. But he also drank and gambled to excess. One night, about three years ago, he emptied the safe and took off for Vegas."

"That's one hell of a story," Jake said, pleased the Judge had stopped by tonight and felt like chatting. "Oh, yes, and just so you know," the Judge added, "The whole Sid thing is a very sensitive subject for both the Old Man and for Pat."

"So, I shouldn't bring it up?"

"No, you shouldn't," the Judge laughed, "and get that shit-eating grin off your face."

Jake took another swig of his drink. "What's with the Dragon Lady?" The Judge obviously knew a lot about the Old Man; maybe he had more insight into Carl's girlfriend too. "Her name is Lucille Harris and they live at her house in Edina. She takes care of him and so Pat puts up with her hanging around the Poodle."

"Well, she's a real pain in the ass, and she gossips and tells Carl everything that happens here. It hasn't been a problem for me so far, but it could be some day."

The Judge said, "Not to worry. Pat thinks you're doing a great job, and you've got George in your corner."

Jake nodded. "Damn right, I'm doing a good job. The only problem is I'm not getting hazard pay."

The Judge chuckled.

Jake continued. "Well, you know, Neal, I've never really thanked you for getting me this . . . I guess you could call it a *job*."

"I told Pat that you were the right guy for the job, Jake," the

Judge explained. "I said you're smart, dependable, and have lots of management experience, although not in the bar business." The Judge guffawed. "I went on and on about you. I had to lift my feet off the floor to avoid all the bullshit I told him about you!" He slapped Jake on the back in his usual jovial manner. "Pat thought I must be kidding about the no-bar experience. He wanted me to describe you, so I told him you were clean-cut, thirty-six years old, and physically fit. And I told him, 'He's better-looking than you are, Pat.'"

Jake snickered. "And that did it? He agreed to interview me?"

"Well, yeah, but I also told him about you being an ex-Marine," the Judge grinned.

"Well, I just wanted to tell you thanks, man"—Jake reached out to shake Neal's hand—"and that it's working out for me here." Then he looked around and noticed that they were getting busy. "I have to go and deal with the huddled masses."

JAKE HAD JUST COME UP FROM the liquor storage room when he noticed an unfamiliar face entering the bar. He was diligent about greeting customers and meeting most of the people that came into the Poodle. It made them feel special.

This new face reminded him of Jack Palance, the actor. Only this guy was the real thing. He stood over six feet, and his ruddy complexion and chiseled features were highlighted by a pair of dark fiery eyes. He looked like he was wired too tightly. One intense, scary-looking dude, Jake thought, as he set down the bottles he'd brought up from below, never taking his eyes off the unknown man.

Jake approached and introduced himself. "Hi, I'm Jake Sherman, the new manager."

"I don't give a fuck who you are. Piss off!"

Jake opened his mouth to say "Fuck you too!" but before he could, George reached over the bar and held up his hand at the other man. "That's enough, Doyle," he growled.

The man glared at George, then turned and stormed out of the place. George turned to move off behind the bar as if nothing happened.

Jake said, "Who was that asshole?"

"That asshole is Lucky Doyle. I told you about him. You don't want to fuck with him," George explained, adding, "He is one mean mother fucker."

Jake was not convinced. "Can you take him, George?" he asked.

"If you haven't figured out by now, I can take anybody. But this guy, after I got done taking him, I'd have to kill him."

Okay, wow, that was enough for him. Doyle must be one bad hombre. Thank God for George, because he was out of his league with this guy.

Later in the evening, George gave Jake the rest of the scoop. "Doyle's a pimp and a drug dealer and has a reputation for beating his women. And the cops think he might have been involved in a murder, but they can't prove it."

Jake said, "So he's a real scumbag. Should I eighty-six him? Why would we want him around here?"

"No," George smiled, shaking his head and looking disgusted. "The only way Pat will let you eighty-six someone is if he can't pay for a drink!"

Good! Because he didn't really want to deal with this character Doyle anyway.

George looked Jake in the eye. "Look, Jake. Doyle doesn't come in here very often and it seems like he already doesn't like you. Leave it be, and when he does come back, just stay far away from him."

Jake agreed wholeheartedly, but he had a bad feeling about Doyle. He had met some pretty nasty characters in this place, but he sensed this guy was different. He exuded evil and Jake felt a chill just thinking about him.

CHAPTER 4

Sunday, February 18

JAKE LEANED ON THE BAR AND slowly sipped a Beam and soda. It was still early and he had time to think. He'd been managing the Poodle for a month and it seemed that he had it somewhat under control.

Sure, there were still fights and other disturbances, but Jake had established a certain order, convincing himself that, in no uncertain terms, the inmates would not run the asylum.

Jake had instituted a set of rules: The criminals could do nothing illegal on the premises—no selling dope, no gambling, no pimping, and no fighting, though that last rule had been only moderately successful.

The hookers were welcome as long as they didn't solicit in the bar.

The cops—and there were plenty that came in off-duty for a drink or two—he let them know he wasn't a snitch and wouldn't do their work for them, with a few notable exceptions of child molesters, pushers, rapists, and murderers.

He had reason to test this theory on Jimmy Box the night Jimmy turned to the guy next to him and smashed him in the mouth. After Jake and Leonard picked the guy up and helped him out the door, Jake sat down on the stool next to Jimmy.

"Listen, Jimmy—"

"Hey, I punched that asshole because—" Jimmy interrupted.

Jake held up his hands, palms out. "I don't want to know. I don't give a shit. Here's the deal, Jimmy," he said. "What you do outside the bar is none of my business. I couldn't care less. You could kill someone, for all I care, as long as you don't do it in the Poodle. However, when you're here, if you pull something like that, I'll have to deal with it. And I don't want to be put in that position, so let's come to an understanding."

Jimmy nodded. "Okay, but let me tell *you* something. The Old Man pours the cheap scotch into my Johnny Walker Red, and in case you don't know it, they call that old fucker the Hennepin Avenue Chemist. I'm goddamned tired of drinking this cheap shit."

Not particularly surprised at the news, Jake gingerly patted Box on the shoulder. "Thanks for telling me. I'm going to look into this."

As he walked away, he heard Jimmy say to George, "I like that guy. He's got some kind of *cajones*, talking to me like that."

When Jake arrived for his shift the next day, he talked to Pat about Carl's tricks with the booze, but Pat only shrugged and said, "He's my father. What can I do?"

JAKE HAD NOTICED A PONG MACHINE when he first started at the Poodle but didn't give it much thought. After a month or so, however, whenever there was a lull in the action, he played the video game machine to keep from getting bored. After putting in several hours on it, he became an expert. He could predict exactly which way the ball would bounce on the screen.

He placed bets with the customers, and even if he hadn't had much to drink, he pretended to be three sheets to the wind so they would think they had the edge. But he always won. The extra money came in handy. He usually gave the extra money to Kelly for the kids, but he never told her he won it hustling Pong.

JAKE INVITED SOME OF HIS FRIENDS to stop by the Poodle for a drink. On Thursday night, Jim Dean came in with John Johnson, two guys who had been in the same insurance office that Jake had worked in before he'd wound up at the Poodle.

He bought them a drink, and they were shooting the shit when a fight broke out across the bar.

Jake ran to break it up, whipping out his club en route. Thankfully, he didn't need to use it as he separated the two schmucks arguing about God knows what.

When he returned to the table where Jim and John sat, they wore shocked looks on their faces.

Jim asked, "Does this happen often?"

Jake answered nonchalantly, "Yeah, we got a problem here almost every evening, but it's nothing I can't handle."

His two friends exchanged a glance. John said, "We gotta be going, Jake. We're supposed to meet some people." They quickly finished their drinks and left.

Jake knew by the expressions on their faces that they wouldn't be back. He shrugged. Oh well, the Poodle wasn't for everyone.

Later on that evening, he called Kelly, just to shoot the breeze. He needed to talk to someone normal, especially after Jim and John bailed on him. It still bothered him that they were put off by him breaking up a fight.

"Hey, Jake," Kelly said after some small talk, "you never told me what the Poodle looks like inside. How big is it?"

"There are actually four rooms in the place," he explained, happy she'd asked. "When you first walk in the front door, there's this huge bar that takes up one room. It's rectangular in shape, with a couple dozen stools scattered around its four sides. To the rear of the bar is seating for an additional thirty people or so. To the right and up two steps is the dining room, which seats approximately sixty. And then there's a room to the left, which seats about fifty and has a small dance floor. We have live music on weekends," he added.

"How's the food?"

"The menu is basically meat and potatoes. Very average."

"Yes, it sounds like it," she replied. "Well, I don't want to be rude, but I need to put the kids to bed, Sherman."

He liked it when she called him Sherman; it meant that she wasn't mad at him.

She added, "Do you want to say hi to them first?"

"Sure, yes. Oh, and one more thing, Kelly . . ."

"What?"

"I love you."

"I know, Jake. I'll put the kids on."

THE NEXT NIGHT, JAKE STAPLED A POSTER to the wall that advertised the new, up-and-coming jazz trio scheduled to play at the Poodle that weekend. Great. It would give him some relief from the loud rock 'n' roll crap playing on the jukebox he was forced to listen to most of the time.

Jake, standing at the bar, asked George for another drink. He lit his cigarette and continued his conversation with one of the regulars.

"Regarding Nixon," Jake said, "it looks like that Watergate break-in is going to end up sinking that asshole." The customer nodded.

George added his two cents' worth as he walked by, "Ah, they are all a bunch of fucking crooks. Put 'em all in jail, every last one of those mother fuckers."

Before Jake could think of something clever to say, the waitress Cindy approached and said, "Jake, we've got a problem. There is a couple of queers dancing together! And the inmates, as you call them, are getting restless."

He sighed, wishing he could have one night of peace in this joint. He enjoyed talking politics with some of the customers. A few of them could actually hold a decent conversation.

He walked over to the room with the dance floor, looked around, and observed that all eyes were on two fags slow dancing. They were the only ones on the floor; everyone else had cleared off. The crowd was muttering and Jake heard an obscenity or two. In another minute, he thought, they will tear this couple apart.

He approached the dancing duo and said, "Look, boys, it doesn't matter to me, but if you don't leave in the next thirty seconds, I won't be responsible for your safety."

The young men broke apart, frowning. One stood with his hands on his hips and started to say something, but Jake cut him off. "Hey, jerkoffs, get the hell out of here, now!" He raised his fist and glared at them, "I'm doing you a favor, so move!"

Someone from the crowd yelled, "You tell 'em, Jake!"

Another person called, "You need any help showing them the door, Jake, you let me know."

They two young men got the message, grabbed their coats off the back of their chairs, and left, once again holding hands. As Jake left the room, some of the inmates cheered him. "Way to go, Jake! You showed them what's right and what's wrong!"

"You can all go fuck yourselves," he said to the crowd in a loud voice. It pissed him off that he'd allowed himself to be swayed by the customers. That wasn't like him. Personally, he didn't really have any feelings one way or the other about people's sexuality; he didn't care what they did.

The incident was over, but Jake couldn't stop thinking about it. He hadn't known many queers in his life; at least not that he knew of. Reggie, the front desk clerk at the Hotel Anthony next door to the Poodle, he was queerer than a two-dollar bill, but he was okay. In the Marine Corps, there had been a kid from North Carolina that seemed light in the loafers. A few guys in the barracks decided to give him the blanket treatment one night, which entailed throwing a blanket over the poor schmuck and beating the hell out of him. The idea was that it helped reduced the number and severity of marks left on the victim. Jake had wanted to stop them, but there were too many guys in on it.

The whole scene with the two fags dancing tonight reminded him of that night in the Marines. He felt real bad about kicking out paying customers who kept to themselves, just because the crowd had egged him on.

By the next evening, Jake had forgotten about the incident. The thermometer read fifteen below zero. Add the wind chill, and the temperature reached minus twenty-five below.

Needless to say, the place was pretty quiet until eight, when the Judge came in and, barely able to contain his laughter, announced, "There are several guys of a certain persuasion outside, carrying signs saying that you are prejudiced against gay people."

"Oh fuck," Jake said. "I hope they freeze out there. "Was there no end to the craziness of the Poodle?

Carl overheard the Judge and announced, "I'll take care of them."

"Be my guest," said Jake. He figured the Old Man would go out there and yell at them.

He should be so lucky. In a few minutes, one of the regulars came in and said to Jake, "Go look outside. You won't believe what's going on out there."

Not the least bit interested in going out in the cold, Jake reluctantly opened the front door and saw the short, gray-haired Old Man using a fire hose on the picketers. Thoughts of Laurel and Hardy came to mind as he said to himself, "Here's another fine mess you've gotten me into."

Jake turned off the hose and yelled at Carl, "Jesus Christ, are you crazy?" He urged the rest of the customers to come back inside.

Showing no remorse, Carl exclaimed, "Now they're like popsicles and they can suck each other off."

Jake closed his eyes in frustration and shook his head. That was actually a pretty funny line. Still, Jake was responsible for what went on at the Poodle, and the Old Man's behavior hadn't been very smart.

Back inside, Carl told the story. Customers slapped him on the back and laughed. Though it was amusing on the one hand, Jake's sensible side was concerned about future repercussions.

The next day proved him right. He grimaced when he saw the front page of the *Minneapolis Star and Tribune*. A reporter had taken a picture of Carl hosing down the picketers.

Jake tossed the paper onto the bar. He had only been at the Poodle less than six weeks, but too many crazy things had happened in that time. Maybe he should start looking for another job. His sanity could be at stake if he hung around here much longer.

CHAPTER 5

Thursday, March 1

Making his rounds in the Poodle, Jake noticed Jose Johnson parked on a seat at the bar.

Jake smiled, recalling a conversation he'd had with George when he'd first started at the Poodle. Jake had overheard a large, middle-aged black man trying to sell a suit to another customer. He asked George what the deal was with the joker peddling clothing in a bar.

George answered, "That's Jose Johnson. He's spent about twenty years, off and on, in prison. He's killed at least four people, and that's not a rumor—that's a fact. He's a legend on Hennepin Avenue. He's semi-retired, and now he's just into fencing an assortment of hot merchandise."

"Doesn't Pat mind that he pulls that shit in here?"

"Mind? Fuck! He buys his suits off of him."

What a bunch of crap! Jake put his hands in his belt, cowboy style, and said with a John Wayne accent, "Well, partner. There's a new sheriff in town, and he won't be selling anything on my watch."

"It's your funeral," George had laughed.

Tonight, Jake strolled over to the bar and nodded a greeting at Jose. He had chatted with him on occasion, letting him know he was welcome in the bar as long as he didn't try to sell stolen goods. "George, pour one on the house for our friend, Jose."

Jose grunted.

That's about all the guy ever says, Jake thought. He just grunts. At least he hasn't been selling shit in here since my come-to-Jesus talk with him. And he'd rather have more people like him than the likes of Lucky Doyle.

ON SATURDAY, JAKE TOOK A CALL from Kelly at the phone behind the bar. "The car insurance is due, Jake. Are you going to pay it or do you expect me to?" she asked.

He told her he'd pay it, and they chatted for a while longer about various subjects.

He finally worked up his nerve and asked her, "So what do you think? Can I come over after work tonight?"

"In your dreams, Sherman!"

Shit. Now what? "Gotta go. Bye."

Jake hung up the phone, his hand still on the receiver. He felt like someone had just dumped a bucket of cold water on him.

George looked at him and noticed his frozen expression. "From the look on your face, you musta been talking to your ex."

"I just can't figure her out. One day she can't wait to see me, and the next she treats me like a leper." He sighed.

George, with the ever-present stupid toothpick sticking out of his mouth, poured him another drink. "Hey, I'm not your fuckin' rabbi. It's not brain surgery. Go pick out some bimbo and get laid."

GEORGE WAS RIGHT. EVEN IF KELLY DIDN'T WANT HIM, there were plenty of other chicks who did. He looked around the bar. The pickings were sometimes slim, but a couple of times a week, a broad appeared that might be worth at least a one-night stand.

Surprisingly enough, broads often felt the same way he did about casual sex. One woman even called it "sport fucking." He grinned and leaned back against the bar. That phrase had legs.

Tonight had potential, he decided as a couple attractive women caught his eye. He planned his move and didn't antici-pate any difficulty.

As he sauntered in the direction of a blonde, he glanced up when the door to the Poodle opened. His friend Marshall Ferster walked in. Jake detoured over to greet him. He'd extended several invitations to his old buddy for a drink at the Poodle. Jake smiled, pleased he'd finally accepted.

They had a few drinks and shot the shit. Fortunately, it was a quiet night.

After a while, Jake got serious. "Here's my dilemma, Marshall. Kelly has cut me off again. I don't want you to think it's only about sex, but when we're on, it feels like there's a chance for getting back together. But now we're off again. So, anyway, for the time being, I'll have to find my action elsewhere. The question is, where do I fuck them? Their place is much too risky. I've had bad experiences with ex-husbands or ex-boyfriends that still have keys to the chick's place."

Marshall looked inquiringly at Jake. "Whoa. Sounds like a good story, man. Tell me about it." He edged forward in his chair and sipped his drink.

"Well, this one time, I was with a broad. We were in her bed, going hot and heavy, and I heard a key in the lock of the door, and I asked her, 'Who in the hell would that be?' She told me, 'That's probably my ex-husband.'

"I sat up and said, 'How big is your ex-husband?' She told me, 'Really big and really mean.'

"I leaped out of bed, pulled on my pants and my shoes, and went out the window. Fortunately, it was on the first floor."

Jake leaned back. "That was a close call. It was a dozen years ago, before I met Kelly, and I learned my lesson then—no screwing at a broad's house."

Marshall shook his head. "Jake, you're my hero," he said wryly. He sipped his drink, then set his glass down. "So, why not go to your house with them?"

Jake shook his head. "Yeah, but then it becomes a problem getting rid of them in the morning. So that's why I'm going to have to have another rule. If they come to my house, they should at least have their own car, because otherwise I would have to get up and drive them home. That's the last thing I want to do in the morning."

He pointed toward the front door. "I could take them next door to the Hotel Anthony, but then I would have to drive all the way out to Wayzata to clean up and change clothes, then come all the way back downtown to work."

"Problems, problems," Marshall mocked him. "Sounds like it's just too damn much trouble. Maybe you could take up masturbating, instead."

"Very fuckin' funny."

Marshall finished his drink. "Well, I have to get home." He stood up, and so did Jake. "Good to see you, Jake."

"Good to see you, too," he said, and stuck out his hand. "Don't be a stranger. Thanks for the whacking-myself suggestion. And up yours, too," he chuckled.

After Marshall left, Jake said to himself, "So, this is my quest: to get laid tonight."

The blonde had already left, so he spent the rest of the evening looking for fresh meat. About midnight, he finally found a live one. He walked up to her. "How about a little sport fucking tonight?"

Either that, he said to himself, or it's gonna be Marshall's suggestion.

FRIDAY AND SATURDAY EVENINGS were generally the busiest and potentially the nights for the most fights. Not from the regulars, but strangers to the Poodle. Jake had talked Pat into hiring a bouncer to help out. It didn't go well with Carl, who didn't want to spend the money. But eventually Pat gave in, and it gave Jake a sense of security having another body around in case of trouble. Jake's ego wanted to handle everything, but in this case his good sense carried the day.

The bouncers were off-duty cops. It was a good gig for them because most of the time they did nothing but drink free booze and pick up chicks. One of the cops, Frank Macpherson, took most of the shifts. Jake liked him; he was tough and pretty sharp.

On the third Saturday in March, about ten o'clock, a newcomer had too much to drink and Jake told him to leave the bar.

"You wanna fight? You wanna try to take me on?" the wiry man belligerently asked a couple of nearby customers, ignoring Jake.

Frank came over. He and Jake each grabbed an arm on the man and walked him out the seldom-used back door.

In the alley, the guy shook free. "I'm warning you, I'm a karate expert," he said, then yelled something neither of them could understand, and assumed a Bruce Lee stance. Without hesitation, Frank kicked him in the balls and Jake hit him with his club.

The poor guy rolled around on the wet pavement, moaning and groaning.

Jake shook his head. "Damn, I didn't get to see his karate moves." Laughing, Jake and Frank walked back into the bar.

Frank put an arm around Jake. "Louie, I think this is the beginning of a beautiful friendship." Jake liked Frank all the more for quoting the famous line.

JAKE CATEGORIZED THE CUSTOMERS into three groups. Actually, four. There were the regulars that came in several times a week. Then the part-timers who came in maybe twice a week. Third were those who were unpredictable—you might not see them for three or four weeks, then they might show up three nights in a row. And fourth were strangers who just came in once and you never saw them again.

Lucky Doyle fit into the third category. Each time he came, which wasn't that often, Jake tensed and didn't let him out of his sight. Jake often caught Doyle watching him out of the corner of his eye, and one time Doyle flipped Jake off when their eyes met. Each time Doyle came in, the situation escalated.

The most recent time Doyle put in an appearance, George said, "Jake, I've told you before and I'll tell you again." Chomping on his toothpick, he planted both hands on the bar and leaned toward Jake. "Just stay away from that mother fucker."

Jake felt his face redden. He pounded on the bar with his fist and replied, "It's a two-way street, George. Keep that mother fucker away from me!"

Jake couldn't help it—he glared at Lucky again.

Doyle looked back at Jake. "What the fuck are you looking at?" He got off his bar stool and headed toward Jake.

Oh shit, Jake thought. Here we go.

Fortunately, Frank was on duty as the bouncer. He quickly stepped in front of Doyle. "Doyle, it's time you left."

Lucky's gaze darted between Jake and Frank, a menacing look on his face. He started to take another step forward.

Frank said in a deep voice, "You really don't want to go there."

Doyle clenched his fists and Jake did the same, ready for whatever happened next. He took a step closer to Frank and Doyle. The bar was quiet as everyone waited to see what Doyle would do.

Lucky took one more look over Frank's shoulders at Jake, then said to Frank, "I don't have any beef with *you*, cop." He turned on his heel and stomped out of the bar.

CHAPTER 6

Wednesday, March 28

J AKE CALLED TO CHECK IN WITH KELLY, to see how she and the children were doing. After some small talk, Kelly said, "Jake, let's get serious for a minute. I had a conversation with Neal Phillips' wife, Judy, the other night. She related that he's noticed a huge change in your demeanor, your personality—"

"What are you talking about?" What the fuck had the Judge said?

"Well, he said you're getting into fights, drinking more, screwing around . . . it's none of my business, but you know I'm concerned. What the hell's going on with you, anyway?"

Jake's temper rose. The last thing he wanted was for Kelly to know what life was like at the Poodle. He forced himself to calm down and sound casual. "Oh, sure, that. Well, once in a great while, there's a confrontation, but it's nothing to get concerned about."

"Hmm. Well, I wondered what the Phillips were talking about because I don't see any of that when you're with me and the kids. It almost sounds as if you're developing a Dr. Jekyll and Mr. Hyde personality, Jake," she said in her half-joking, half-serious voice. "Be careful that the distinction doesn't become blurred."

Jake tried to make light of it. "Well, my dear," he drawled in a deep, inviting voice, "which one would you prefer?"

THE NEXT FRIDAY EVENING, things were calm until a call came in about eleven.

Jake answered. "Poodle."

"Are you the manager?" a male voice asked.

"Yeah, what do you want?"

"I'm going to kill you tonight."

It took a moment for the words to sink in. Jake had had other calls that were weird, but none like this. His temper rose.

"Listen, you fuck," he said impatiently. "I will be leaving here about one-thirty and I'll be wearing a tan raincoat. Come and get me, cocksucker."

Jake slammed the phone down and immediately relayed the conversation to George and Frank.

"It's probably just a crank call," Frank said, "but just in case, I'll hang around after closing."

When the time came, George decided to join Frank in seeing Jake safely to his car. Jake closed up the Poodle, set the alarm, and three of them went out the back door—George on his left and Frank on the right. Both of them had their guns drawn.

Jake thought, this is like a B movie.

Nothing happened.

Jake unlocked his car, checked the back seat, and got inside. He waved to Frank and George as they headed to their cars.

On the way home, Jake said to himself, "What have you learned tonight, Sherman?"

He answered himself immediately. "This is fucking nuts, that's what I've learned. I need to get out of that place."

JAKE STOOD AT THE BAR. *He gulped down what he thought was a Beam and soda.*

Suddenly, he shuddered and his whole body shook. His skin grew tight and hot, and rage coursed through him.

He looked down at his hands—they were gnarly and hairy and large. His claw-like fingers were bending into fists. The fingernails were long and sharp.

He looked up in the mirror on the wall across the room. A

grotesque face looked back at him.

The creature's body was growing out of its clothes. Jake felt his shirt and jacket ripping. The creature growled and Jake realized the sound had come from him. He let out an earth-shattering scream and ran out of the bar to avoid what he saw in the mirror.

He ran until he ended up in a dark alley. A young woman exited a door at the back of a store. She saw Jake and screamed . . . to no avail. He attacked her.

His attention was drawn to another young woman in the alley. He dropped the first woman's lifeless body, grabbed the second woman and attacked her too.

A crowd had gathered at the end of the alley. They chanted, "Get the monster! Get him!"

He dropped his second victim and ran.

The crowd was closing in on him. Closer . . . closer . . .

He woke up, bathed in sweat. The sheets were twisted around his legs and he kicked himself free. Shaking, he looked at his hands—they looked normal.

He stumbled out of bed and made a beeline for the bathroom. He gripped the countertop and stared into the mirror. His face looked normal too. He nearly collapsed in relief.

"Fuck. Was that a dream? It felt so real." He blinked a few times to clear his vision. He was still sweating and breathing heavily. "It really felt real. Maybe it was. After all, Dr. Jekyll didn't know at first that he was turning into Mr. Hyde," he laughed but not convincingly.

He splashed cold water on his face and tried to calm his racing heart. He took a deep breath, then exhaled slowly.

"Hell. Whether it was real or not, Kelly was right—I'm turning into something I'm not, at least in my dreams," he told his reflection.

He shook his head to clear it and took another deep breath. He felt calmer now, more in control. "Nah. It was just a nightmare. It wasn't real, and I'm fine. Kelly said she hasn't noticed any change in me. I can handle the Poodle. I can keep the Poodle separate from the rest of my life. I'm fine."

So far, a little voice whispered back.

CHAPTER 7

Monday, April 2

Jake couldn't shake his Jekyll and Hyde dream. It haunted him and played on his fears that Kelly—and the Judge—had a point about his job at the Poodle coloring his view of reality. He ran into a lot of mean characters at the Poodle. Maybe it was time to do something about it.

One night after work, as he had breakfast with George, he said seriously, "George, I've given it a lot of thought, and I need to get a gun."

George narrowed his gaze. "You know, Jake, there's more to a gun than just owning one. If you don't know how to use the goddamned thing, you'll end up shooting your pecker off."

"Fuck you very much. I know how to use a goddamned gun. I was in the Marine Corps," he shot back, "and I actually qualified as expert with my M1 rifle."

They were quiet for a minute as the waitress came over and topped off their coffee.

George took a sip, then set the cup down. "Well, what about pistols?"

"Well, I did fire a .45, but my results were . . . less than perfect," Jake said tongue in cheek.

George pushed his empty plate away. "You know, if we both have guns, we might end up shooting each other."

"You don't have to worry. Remember, I told you I was a bad shot," he laughed at the absurd idea. "But all kidding aside, I *am* going to get a gun on my next day off."

"Well, okay, if you made up your mind, I'm sure I can't talk you out of it." George leaned forward. "You oughta go to a gun store and buy the damn thing. I would recommend the same one I'm carrying—a .38. It's small, easy to conceal, and has enough pop to do the job."

If it was good enough for George, it should be good for him. "Okay, George, because when I grow up, I want to be just like you."

JAKE WAS CURIOUS BY NATURE. HE had been working at the Poodle for three months and still didn't understand what was up with the Hotel Anthony, which was adjacent to the Poodle. Pat and Carl owned the hotel too. From time to time he saw people going in the Anthony that looked familiar. He thought he had seen them in the newspapers. A congressman, a judge—he couldn't be sure who they were.

Even though Jake was technically in charge of the Anthony, he only went there when a problem arose. Mainly, to handle some drunk who got out of line or someone trying to skip out on paying the bill.

He had asked Pat a few times about what went on over there but only received vague answers. The last time he'd asked, Pat had said to him in a not-so-friendly way, "You know, Jake, there's a need to know . . . and you don't need to know."

Now for sure, he thought, I've going to find out what's going on.

George wasn't much help. He did say that there were some high-stakes poker games and, of course, people got laid. But Jake knew George well enough by now to know that he didn't give a shit about what was going on over there, so he'd be no help.

On a quiet evening in early April, after he knocked back a couple of drinks, and out of sheer boredom, he strolled into the hotel to have a conversation with Reggie, the front desk clerk/manager. Reggie was an inch or two taller than Jake, skinny, and wore glasses. His long blonde hair brushed the top of shoulders. He had a high-pitched voice and a prissy little walk. He was, as Jake liked to say, light in the loafers.

His curiosity at an all-time high, he got right to the point. "Reggie, I'm here to find out all the dirty secrets regarding this poor excuse for a hotel."

"I don't know what you're talking about." Reggie waved him off with an effeminate gesture.

"If you don't fill me in, the next time you have a guest who gets three sheets to the wind, you're shit out of luck."

Reggie's shoulders sagged. "Oh Jake, why do you have to be so mean?"

Jake's pleasant buzz turned to anger. He was fed up of being left out of the loop. And now Reggie was accusing him of being mean. He grabbed Reggie by his tie. "Listen, you fruit of the loom, you are out of time, so talk to me."

"Okay, okay," he whined, "what do you want to know?" Jake let him go and waited impatiently.

Just then, one of the Poodle customers came running in the front door. "Jake, George said to come back right now."

Fuck. Right when he was about to get some answers. Jake started to leave, stopped, and said to a relieved Reggie, "To be continued."

He nodded glumly and Jake took off for the Poodle. "I'll catch up with you real soon, Reggie," he said over his shoulder.

A FEW DAYS LATER, Jake went downtown early in the afternoon to look for a gift for his daughter Sarah's eleventh birthday, which was coming up on April twenty-third. He shopped at Dayton's and found a nice blouse and jeans. Jake would be unable to attend her party because he had to work. He felt terrible but had promised her that they would celebrate when she and Sean stayed over with him, on his next night off.

He didn't want to drive all the way back home to Wayzata so he decided to go to the Poodle, have lunch, and hang out. He didn't have anywhere else to go, and at least at the Poodle, he would know someone. The daytime customers, however, were a lot different from the nighttime crowd; they were mostly business types and so there very few, if any, problems.

Pat was there, though, doing his schtick—going up and down the bar and over to the neighboring tables, greeting people, slapping them on the back, and occasionally signaling the daytime bartender for a drink on the house. When Jake had initially interviewed for the job, he'd watched Pat's friendly jocularity and had wondered if the same would be expected of him—which he had found a bit disconcerting as he considered himself an introvert and not the glad-handing type.

As Pat joked around with a couple of guys in business suits, Jake realized he'd developed his own friendly style with customers—and it was working just fine. No need to mimic Pat's routine.

He turned his attention to the grilled liver and onions the waitress set before him, and dug in. The Poodle's food was filling and some of it wasn't half bad. Pat stopped by his table to shoot the breeze but soon got called away.

Ten minutes later, as Jake finished his lunch, the hostess approached and said, "Jake, the daytime desk clerk at the Anthony called and told me that Pat's gone up to one of the rooms to collect from a guest. The desk clerk thought that there might be trouble."

Jake shot out of his chair and told the hostess to get Henry, the cook. Henry weighed in at least two hundred sixty pounds and was well over six feet. Even better, he wielded a big butcher knife. Jake felt that between the two of them, they could handle any problem—this wouldn't be the first time he and Henry had teamed up.

When they arrived in the lobby of the Anthony, they saw Pat racing down the stairs, chased by a disheveled man with a crazed look in his eye.

Pat cried out, "I maced myself, I maced myself!" He had one hand covering his eyes and the other holding the banister as he stumbled downs the stairs. Jake thought he was watching a Mack Sennet comedy. He tried hard not to laugh but was not very successful.

Pat reached the bottom of the stairs and Henry knew what to do: he stepped between Pat and the fool chasing him. One look at Henry and his butcher knife, and the man came to a dead stop and turned to flee back up the stairs.

Jake called out loudly, "If we have to come up after you, I promise that you will be visiting the emergency room or the morgue."

The guy paused, turned, and came back down the stairs. He sheepishly asked the clerk how much he owed, settled his bill, and left.

Back at the bar when Pat had washed the mace out of his eyes, Jake said, "If I were you, I would choose another weapon of choice." He grinned.

Pat snorted. "Fuck you and the horse you rode in on."

Jake just shook his head. This story had legs and would be good for laughs for at least a week. He still had an hour to kill before his shift and decided this would be a good time to finish his conversation with Reggie, who he knew was just coming on duty.

The timing should be perfect, Jake thought, because the daytime desk clerk would undoubtedly tell Reggie about the recent confrontation. He would be scared, and Jake figured this would soften him up so he'd be more forthcoming about what really went on at the Anthony.

When Reggie saw him, he said, "Hey, man, thanks for helping out today. I don't know what the clerk would have done if you and Henry hadn't shown up."

Jake leaned on the counter. "You were going to give me the lowdown on this place the other evening. Is this a good time?"

"Okay, but if you ever tell anybody, it could mean my job, or worse." He glanced left and right, but no one was within hearing distance.

Jake's curiosity grew. His thoughts had centered the past few days around two things: the gun he needed to buy and the juicy hotel gossip he needed to hear. He impatiently drummed his fingers on the counter, raised an eyebrow, and waited.

Reggie sighed. "Fine. First of all, you have to understand that the main reason the customers I'm going to tell you about come here is because they count on our discretion."

"Yeah, yeah, come on, will ya? Spit it out." If Reggie didn't start talking soon, Jake would wring his fucking neck.

"Well, there are some high-stakes poker games that go on upstairs with some local judges, city officials, and high-profile businessmen."

"Shit, that's not so terrible. What else?"

"Well, then there's the sex," Reggie added.

When Jake heard the word sex, he perked up. Hmm, he thought, this will hopefully get more interesting. He urged Reggie to continue.

"Some of the same types of people I mentioned bring women to the rooms. Some of these guys even bring—well, you know—other men to the room. I'm also aware of some drug deals that have gone down but I couldn't swear to that."

"That's very interesting, but can you tell me *who* these people are? Names, Reggie, I want names," Jake insisted.

Reggie whined, "Why do you want them?"

"A wise man once told me that knowledge is power, and I'm a naturally curious guy. Who knows, someday I—" Jake decided not to continue, worried that Reggie wouldn't name names if Jake said any more. Jake didn't plan on doing anything with the information, but it was always a good idea to have the dirt on someone and thus the upper hand.

Reggie finally coughed up the names of a few people. Jake was surprised at what he heard. Bigwigs, indeed.

Jake leaned across the counter and patted Reggie on the cheek. "You're a prince—or a princess. Whatever."

Jake walked back into the Poodle and immediately noticed a scary-looking tough dude leaning over the bar, talking to George. Jake got within hearing distance but didn't interrupt the guy, who was built like a gorilla.

"Listen, Christenson," the ape-man ground out, "that fucker Doyle owes me a lot of bread. You tell him the next time you see him that Dutch is gonna nail his hide to the wall."

"Hey, I'm not a fuckin' messenger," George said.

The two glared at each other. Not surprisingly, George didn't back down in the least.

The guy shrugged, downed his drink, and left the bar without leaving a tip.

Jake asked George, "What was that all about?"

"That was Dutch Lundgren, the other badass I told you about. Just another fucker who's been screwed by Doyle."

JAKE SHARED HIS PLAN TO GET a gun with anyone that would listen. After all, his life had been threatened. He knew that most of them were idle threats by people who were drunk and probably harmless. Nevertheless, you couldn't be too careful. Each night, when he routinely closed up and left the place around 2 a.m., he felt completely vulnerable while he walked the block to his car. And especially on the Sundays when George was off and that punk Nick was bartending. The death threat phone call had shaken him a bit, and the Jekyll and Hyde dream had been the final straw.

One early spring evening, Jake was telling customer Harry Gruber about his need to get a gun.

George interrupted. "Jake, you bitch as much as my ex old lady!" Jake hadn't been aware of complaining, so, then and there, he decided to stop procrastinating and buy the damn gun.

As fate would have it, the very next evening one of the regulars, Alvin Larson, approached Jake and said in a low voice, "I brought a gun for you. Let's go to the office where there is some privacy."

Stunned that this guy would offer him a gun, Jake was a bit suspicious. Alvin was a regular, but he had barely talked to him other than to say hello. He tried to recall any conversation of substance; he could only remember talking to him about current movies playing at the Orpheum, and general bullshit.

In the office, Alvin showed him the gun. "This is a 1940 Smith & Wesson .357 Magnum with a four-inch barrel." He caressed it. "Notice the ivory grips, which, by themselves, are worth more than the gun. It has a capacity of six rounds." He reached into a bag and pulled out two items. "Here's a box of bullets, and a shoulder holster."

Jake was intrigued but concerned about the price. "How much do you want for it?"

"I'm not selling it; I'm letting you use it for as long as you like." He then explained to Jake that he was a gun collector and had plenty of others, and added, "I assume that you know how to handle a revolver."

Jake nodded. "When I was in the Marine Corps I qualified expert with a M1 rifle. The only pistol I fired was a .45, though, and I couldn't hit the broadside of a barn." Jake turned the gun over in his hands, getting a feel for it. "But Al, I have to ask, why so generous?"

Al replied, "I've been coming here for a long time, and I admire the way you've taken charge. I feel safer with you here. You don't take any shit from anyone, and you're just an overall stand-up guy, Jake." He added, "So, don't worry about the recoil on this gun. It's nothing like a .45 has."

Wow. He really had a gun. He hefted its weight in his right hand. For a 1940 gun, it looked, for all practical purposes, new. The silver metal gleamed.

Al said, "I typed up some instructions for you, too, on how to clean it. Here," he said, and handed Jake a folded piece of paper.

He thanked Larson and said, "From now on, pal, your money's no good at the Poodle."

Jake strapped on the gun and couldn't wait to show George. Several times that evening he went to the office and tried taking it out of the holster in front of the mirror. He sucked at it. His moves were jerky and not at all fluid or quick. It wasn't like in the movies; he would need lots of practice. Jake pointed the gun in the mirror and said, *Bang, Bang.* He laughed.

The next day he woke up early, anxious to practice getting the gun out of his holster with ease and without shooting himself. He stood in front of the mirror and, after several tries, gave up. He kept catching his thumb on the flap of the holster as he withdrew the gun. He vowed to practice every day until he perfected the draw.

That evening at work he thought about what would happen if he had to actually use the gun to shoot someone. Many years ago when he was in the Marine Corps, he had been put on guard duty a month before his discharge. His job was to escort inmates to and from the brig. Some were violent criminals. At the time, he had thought long and hard and decided that if it were necessary, he could pull the trigger.

So why was he having second thoughts about carrying this weapon now? The answer was obvious; no matter what the circumstances were, he would be in trouble if he ever used it. Even shooting someone in self-defense created a whole slew of problems. What if he hit an innocent bystander, or actually killed someone? Yeah, he had lots to think about.

One thing he had to do right away was to get a license to carry the gun.

He went to the Hennepin County Courthouse the next day and filled out the application.

Where it asked for the reason, he thought, What a stupid question. His life had been threatened. Why else would he need a gun? He wrote, "My life has been threatened."

He was pissed off when a few days later he received a letter rejecting his application. That evening he vehemently complained to George and the regulars seated around the bar. "Can you fucking believe this shit? How goddamned dumb are the city officials?"

Frank MacPherson had stopped in for a drink with another cop. He told Jake to cool down. "Look, here's how you get the license. Go back, fill out another app, and tell them that you are required as part of your job to carry large amounts of cash daily, to deposit at the bank."

Bingo. The application was approved immediately. Jake laughed to himself. Money was more important than his life. Go figure!

A few evenings later, Jake left the Poodle around 2 a.m. He had had quite a bit to drink—more than usual—and was feeling no pain as he crossed the parking lot, heading for his car. Suddenly someone grabbed him on his right from behind. As he turned and instinctively punched with his left, he thought his next move should be to use his other hand to pull out the gun.

But the moment his left hand made contact with his assailant, excruciating pain radiated through his hand and up his arm. His fist had connected with something much more solid than some asshole's face.

"Oh fuck! What have I done?" he cried, doubling over in pain.

He realized what had happened. His trench coat had caught on the fender of a car and he had punched the goddamned thing. "I could've killed a car if I had gotten the goddamned gun out."

He sat down on the ground and didn't know whether to laugh or cry, but because the pain in his hand was unbearable, he cried.

CHAPTER 8

Wednesday, April 11

Somehow he got home. In the morning the pain was worse. His hand was so swollen he could barely get his shirt on.

He went to the emergency ward at one of the local hospitals and was told him he had fractured two metacarpals.

"In English," he asked.

"Okay, you fractured two knuckles."

"Well, that's going to fuck me up."

They put his hand in a cast, almost up to his elbow, then gave him a shot, lots of pain pills, and sent him on his way.

As Jake drove downtown to work, he looked at the cast on his left hand and thought, What the hell, another weapon.

Jake sat on the can. Two o'clock in the morning and Kelly had waited up for him. When she'd heard about his cast, she took pity on him and had invited him over. *Life is good*, he thought. He'd take a shower and then they'd make passionate love.

His thoughts were interrupted when Kelly called from the bedroom, in a firm but controlled voice, "You better get in here."

"What's the matter?" he laughed. "You can't wait?"

Once again and this time with less control, she said, "Jake, you better get in here right now!"

"Jesus, Kelly, I haven't showered yet."

"Jake, for Christ's sake, get in here!" she shouted. "There is a man trying to climb in our window."

He rushed in and saw a hand disappearing in the dark. His gun—where the hell was it when he needed it? He had left it locked in the Mustang's glove box, and he wouldn't have time to get it if he wanted to catch the man who'd tried to sneak in.

Without taking any time to think, he ran out of the bedroom and took the stairs four at a time. Dashing through the kitchen, he grabbed a large knife and flung open the back door.

He spotted the man running down the street and took off after him. Adrenaline surged through him. When he caught the pervert, he would castrate him.

Suddenly, Jake stopped, aware that he was stark naked. For sure, Kelly would've called the cops and they would see him racing down the street, wearing nothing, and carrying a large knife.

He hurried back to the house. Kelly confirmed that she had called the law.

With a straight face, he asked, "Are we still on for tonight?"

WHEN HE CAME TO WORK THE NEXT DAY, Pat told him that he was going to stay late so that Jake and George could go collect money from the deadbeats who had stiffed them with bad checks.

Jake nodded. What the hell. This would be entertaining, although he wished he had two good hands. He was still getting used to his cast.

Jake drove one-handed, his bad hand cradled on his lap. George clued him in on the procedure.

"Jake, let me do the talking. You watch my back and put your gun in your belt in the front so that they can see you're carrying."

The first stop was Fuzzy Warbles. As they entered the bar, Jake noticed he and George were the only white faces in the place. George knew the bartender, Ned, and after saying hello and doing a little bullshitting, George asked casually, "Is Raymond around?"

About six-and-a-half feet tall, with the muscles to match, Ned looked like a black Paul Bunyan. He apparently knew without being told why we were there.

Ned turned his head slightly and indicated with his eyes that the deadbeat Raymond was in the back room. George and Jake ambled in that direction. All eyes followed them. Jake broke out in a sweat. George nudged Jake and inclined his head. "That's the guy over there, playing pool."

Raymond looked up and said, "Well, lookee who's here. George, you jive ass mother fucker. And who is that little white mother fucker with the crippled hand covering your back?"

George ignored the remarks. "Listen, you fuckin' asshole. We are here to collect on the checks you bounced, plus twenty for our time and trouble. If you don't hand over a hundred bucks right now, I'm going to beat the shit out of you and then turn your sorry ass upside down and shake the money out."

Holy shit.

Raymond's eyes got big. "Hey, hey, man, I don't want any trouble." He handed over the money.

Jake followed George out of the bar, walking backwards, his eye on Raymond and everyone else.

They made three more stops, collecting at two of them. Their man wasn't at the last place, so they called it quits for the night.

George handed Jake thirty dollars and said, "That's your share. We split fifty, fifty. Not bad for an hour of nothing."

"That's easy for you to say," Jake said, wishing he had a clean shirt to put on. He'd sweated through what he was wearing.

They came back to the Poodle. Pat went home and Jake downed his first drink of the night. "This is total bullshit. I wasn't hired to be a fucking bill collector!" Jake said to George, who shrugged. Jake held up his empty glass. "Keep 'em coming."

The place was busy. Every bar stool was occupied. George was filling orders and had his back to the side of the bar where Jake was standing, downing another drink.

Suddenly a customer pulled out a large knife, waved it around in the air, and shouted something unintelligible at George.

Still feeling the rush of the earlier confrontations with the deadbeats, Jake leaped into action. He withdrew his gun without thinking and came up on the man from behind, then jammed the pistol against the crazy bastard's ear. "This is a .357 magnum and if you so much as breath or blink, I'm going to blow your fucking head off. Now put the knife down."

The man froze and dropped the knife.

George was already calling the cops and within minutes they were hauling the fool away.

George poured him another drink and Jake took a swig. He hadn't debated about what to do when he'd seen the knife; he'd just reacted.

One of the customers—a petty crook—asked George if Jake would've really pulled the trigger.

George grinned and replied, "Why don't you give him a reason to find out, you fuckin' asshole."

On his way home that night, Jake almost wished the guy had kept swinging the knife when Jake had the gun to his head. He would have liked to know if he'd have pulled the trigger.

That thought was sobering, and he chastised himself. His life was spinning out of control. What the hell was wrong with him? Was this the Mr. Hyde in him coming out? He shivered.

A FEW MINUTES BEFORE NOON on the following day, Jake found a parking spot a block away from Harry's Café. He was meeting his friend, Jim Dean. He'd been pleasantly surprised when Jimmy telephoned and invited him to lunch.

As he jogged toward the café through a spring downpour, he thought about Jimmy and his wife, Rose. Jake had met them in 1970, when he started selling insurance and the two men worked in the same office. He and Kelly had socialized with them a few times before the divorce. Since then, but before starting his job at the Poodle, he had spent several evenings with them, lamenting how unhappy and empty his life had become without Kelly and the children. Rose always consoled him while Jim told him to quit feeling sorry for himself and get on with his life. He and Jim argued a great deal about politics. Jim, being an archconservative, and Jake, a left-leaning liberal, made for some heated discussions. Still he admired and, yes, envied Jim's life. Rose and Jimmy had four children and were what he called straight-arrow citizens. The guy had been with the same insurance company for fifteen years and had no thought of ever changing.

As Jake did with most of his friends lately, he and Jimmy talked on the phone every couple of weeks, but hadn't gotten together since that night in January when Jimmy and John had come by the Poodle—and not stayed very long. He was still disappointed. After all, there were worst places than the Poodle, weren't there?

When Jake arrived, Jim was already at the table. They shook hands and ordered a drink, then told the waitress they wanted the chicken livers, a popular dish at Harry's Café and a favorite of both of them.

After the usual small talk and kidding each other, Jim became serious. "Jake, I don't know if you're aware, but I've talked to Gary and some of our other friends, and we've noticed quite a change in you since you started working in that place."

"What the fuck are you talking about?" Here's another one that's busting my chops, he thought angrily.

Jim smiled. "That's what I'm talking about. Do you hear yourself? Every sentence contains 'fuck' or some other obscenity. Your whole demeanor has changed and we're worried about you. This isn't like the Jake we knew."

The waitress came over and they both ordered another drink.

When she left, Jim started in again. "I mean, look at you. You told me you're carrying a gun and I see your hand is in a cast—probably from a fight. Jake, what's going on with you?"

Jake started to give his standard rationalization, but Jim interrupted him.

"Listen, Jake, I told Rose I was going talk to you and she said to take it easy, but as you know, I always say exactly what's on my mind. I worry that you are going to end up killing someone with that gun or getting killed. And we care what happens to you. You really need to grow up and stop playing Cowboys and Indians."

Jake leaned back, crossed his arms, and tried to think of a clever response, but he knew Jim was right: He'd become a little rougher around the edges since working at the Poodle, but he'd had to, in order to survive working there. He sighed. "I know you mean well, Jim, and I really appreciate your concern. What I really need to do is find another job."

He added, "There. I just said two complete sentences and I didn't say 'fuck' once."

AFTER LUNCH, HE WALKED OVER TO the Poodle, even though he knew he'd be early for his shift.

The lunch crowd was gone, and Pat was in the office, counting up the lunch receipts. Jake greeted him and said, "Got a minute?"

"Sure. Sit down, take a load off. How's the hand?"

"That's what I've been meaning to ask you. Should I file a workman's comp claim, or does your hospitalization insurance with the Poodle cover this?" He held up his cast.

"I didn't tell you to break your hand," Pat retorted with a smirk.

"Are you fucking kidding me?"

Pat raised his hands, palms outward, as if to calm Jake down. "I'm just messing with ya. When you get all the bills together, just bring them in. I'll take care of it."

Jake was relieved and leaned back in his chair. "Okay, thank you very much. I appreciate that." It would have taken him months to pay off the hospital bill.

Pat said, "Say, I've been meaning to talk to you about Lucky Doyle. What's the deal with you two? He came in the other day and, man, does he have a hard on for you. He was pissing and moaning non-stop about you."

Holy shit. Here was another one on his case. Jake's dander was up. "The deal is, he's a complete asshole. And the less I see of him, the better." He stood up, having had enough of this conversation, then strode back to the kitchen, grabbed a cup of coffee, and sat down in the empty dining room. He lit a cigarette. After a couple of drags, he felt a little calmer, although his thoughts still centered on Lucky Doyle and what a pain in the ass he was. Now the guy was bad-mouthing him to his boss. Chalk one up for the opposition, Jake thought grimly. He wanted to retaliate, just to show Doyle he couldn't be messed with, but it would require some thought. He pictured several scenarios, each one more violent than the other.

He stubbed out his cigarette and leaned back in his chair. "This thing with Doyle is going to come to a head at some point. I can feel it. This is not good."

KELLY CALLED JAKE AT THE POODLE on the following Monday night. He tried to make small talk about the great weekend he'd just had with the kids, but she wasn't having any of it. "I'm not in the mood for that. I want to talk about your gun."

Shit. He tried to make light of it. "Oh, my . . . *gun?*" he said suggestively.

"This isn't a joke. I'm not in the mood for your half-ass humor. The children told me they saw a gun when they were with you at your house. What's the story?"

"It's no big deal. It's just for show. I would never use it," he said magnanimously.

She sighed. "Jake, what the hell is the matter with you. I'm disgusted. Why don't you grow up!" She slammed the phone down.

Shit. Busted again.

"George, get me a drink."

JAKE HAD HAD THE CAST FOR almost two weeks. It didn't hurt all the time but when it did, he just popped a few pain pills the doctor had supplied. Normally, Jake used his left hand for shaving and writing and eating. Using his right hand to shave led to terrible results—he managed to cut himself almost every day. This grew increasingly frustrating, to say the least, and he counted the weeks until he could get the cast off.

That evening, he had to break up a fight in the bar between two regulars arguing about the Minnesota Twins. Thinking he had done so, he turned to walk away. Suddenly one of the combatants took a swing at Jake.

Jake saw red. He blocked the blow with his cast and threw his right, connecting with the sucker's jaw.

The man went down like a ton of bricks, and Jake's right hand throbbed.

George, watching the scuffle, said, "Now that's what I'm talking about. Jake, you're the man!"

But which man—Jekyll? Or Hyde? Jake thought wryly.

One of the customers picked up on George's comment and echoed, "Jake's the man." Soon the entire bar was chanting and banging their glasses. "Jake's the man! Jake's the man!"

Jake raised his hands like a prize fighter. His wrist ached like a sonofabitch. Their accolades didn't go very far toward numbing the pain.

By the time his shift ended, Jake's right wrist had swelled to twice its size and hurt like hell.

The next morning it was even more swollen. The pain brought tears to his eyes. "Oh, fuck, not again!" Jake yelled to his empty house. "How could this be happening to me?"

Once more Jake drove himself to the emergency room, the pain excruciating as he tried to drive with one hand in a cast and the other one perhaps broken.

By chance, he was examined by the same intern, and a very attractive nurse he'd never seen before.

She asked, "What do you do for a living? I hope you get hazard pay."

His first thought was to give her a wise-ass response but, never one to miss an opportunity to hustle, he said, "I manage a bar called the Poodle, downtown. Would you like to come by tonight and have a drink?"

"I'd love to have a drink with you, Jake. Will I be safe?" she winked.

Her eager interest helped Jake take the bad news that he had broken his wrist and would have to have it put into a cast.

Now Jake realized several major problems. First, he would have a difficult time getting his suit or sport coat on with both hands in casts. And if he couldn't, it meant he couldn't hide the gun.

Second, and of equal importance, was that it would be a pain in the butt to light a cigarette.

Even worse, he would have to sip his drinks through a straw since he doubted he could hold a glass. He could just imagine the shit he would get from everyone.

JAKE TRIED AS BEST AS HE COULD to adjust to having casts on both hands. He needed one of the waitresses to light his cigarettes, but at least he could lift his drink with both hands and forego the dreaded straw. He gave the gun to George and told him to keep it under the bar. "If I need to use it, just throw it to me."

"You are one dumb fuck. How do you expect to use it with those pussy bandages?"

After George stopped laughing, they decided that Jake should just try to stay out of trouble for a while. George would do the heavy work and Jake would try talking to patrons rather than getting into fights with them.

Later on that evening the nurse from the Emergency Room came in. Jake had been impressed with her looks that morning, but now in her civvies, she was stunning. About five foot six, maybe 120 pounds. She had beautiful skin, like Kelly, only darker. The ass and legs had attracted him. He wasn't much of a tit man, but long legs, oh boy.

He snapped out of it and bought her a drink. She gave him a brief synopsis of herself, which included her age—twenty-eight—that she was a native Minnesotan, and the fact that she was presently unattached. Jake pretended to be listening, but in reality he was thinking if there was any chance he could get laid tonight.

She must've been reading his mind, because she said, "Why don't you come over after work. You look like you could use some tender loving care." She gave him her address and a key and told him to wake her. Going to her house would mean breaking one of his rules. But, what the hell, rules were made to be broken, he rationalized, especially in a case like this.

After she left, Jake shouted above the noisy crowd, "Once again, thank you, God!"

SHE WAS TERRIFIC IN BED and because of his current condition, she did all the work.

Hooking up with someone wasn't without problems, he was reminded. Sleeping at this girl's place verified the problems, as he'd told Marshall, that went with getting laid. Not only did it take

Jake a full hour to get home, but then he had to figure out how to shower without getting water on the casts.

"What the hell," he growled, and grabbed the plastic that covered his shirts from the cleaners. "I should have showered at her place. She's a goddamned nurse, after all, and could have helped me with this."

Tomorrow night, he vowed, then grinned as the hot water sluicing over his aching body brought a new thought. He had all day to fantasize about the fun they'd have in her bed and her shower tomorrow night.

Their relationship, if you could call it that, lasted a few weeks. She wanted more than he was willing to give and so she dumped him.

It was okay. He was more than ready to move on anyway. Kelly was warming up to him again and he hoped for an invitation to sleep over soon.

But that's as far as it went. Once again, he was down in the dumps.

A FEW NIGHTS LATER, JAKE NOTICED THAT one of the hookers, Sylvia, with whom he had become friendly had come into the Poodle and was seated at the far end of the bar. He liked her because she was smarter than the other pros and wasn't bad looking. Also, she respected his rules: No hustling in the bar.

"Jake, you good-looking devil, sit down and talk to me," she said as she patted the stool next to her. "Most nights lately, you're in a shitty mood, but tonight, you look downright nasty."

What the hell. It was slow tonight. And she was right—he was in a shitty mood. Jake sat and asked George to give them both a drink.

Sylvia asked, "So what's got you so pissed off?"

"You mean in addition to having goddamned casts on both of my hands?" he grumbled.

She nodded sympathetically.

"Okay, fine. It's my ex-wife. I just got off the phone with her and she was busting my balls again." He gulped his drink. Sylvia kept pace with him.

"Why do you keep messing around with her? And, incidentally, how long have you been divorced?"

Jake didn't respond except to order more drinks for both of them. "And make mine a double—and bring me two of them," he told George.

Sylvia said, "You know, I can never be sure when something I say will set you off. So, do you want to continue with this conversation, Jake?"

He shrugged noncommittally, then quickly downed both drinks. "Did I ever tell you how I met Kelly?" he asked morosely.

"No, but I have the feeling you're going to tell me now." Sylvia smiled encouragingly.

Jake started talking, not caring whether she was listening or if she could even hear his mumbled words. "It was the summer of 1961. My friend, Burt Grossman, was going with her. He had to go to National Guard camp for two weeks and at the same time I had some friends visiting from San Francisco. I asked him if it was all right for me to bring Kelly along to make a foursome." Shaking his head, he continued, "I swear I didn't have any ulterior motives."

Jake paused long enough to order another drink. By now, he'd forgotten about Sylvia, and continued his story to himself, staring into space. "She was bright, funny, and beautiful. She wore her red hair long. Her skin was white, and she had the clearest complexion—she still does. Her body is perfectly proportioned." He sipped on his drink when it arrived. "You know, redheads are either good looking, or dogs," he said to no one in particular. "This girl was *really* good-looking."

He fumbled with his pack of cigarettes, inept as always because of the casts. Remembering that Sylvia was there, he handed her the package and asked her, "Light me, will ya? I'm fucking helpless."

"You're mumbling, and I can't understand a word you're saying, Jake," she said, but figured it out anyway and then lit one for herself.

He took a drag on his cigarette, then cleared his throat and tried to pick up where he'd left off. "At the end of two weeks, we had to decide which one of us would tell Burt that we were in love."

Jake knew he was beginning to slur his words. He said to George, "George, help me out here, will ya?"

George leaned over the bar and said, "I'll finish the story. I practically know it by heart because I've heard it enough fuckin' times. He actually met Kelly earlier at a party at his apartment. This guy Burt had brought her. Jake got very drunk and said to another friend, 'See that girl, the one with the red hair? Someday I'm going to marry her!'"

Jake grinned and said, "And that's all f-f-folks."

CHAPTER 9

Thursday, April 26

JAKE PERIODICALLY CALLED KELLY TO CHECK in on her and the kids, and also to try to determine if she was seeing someone and how often. He was pretty sure she was, from some things the kids had said. And she was evasive on the phone when he tried to get her to tell him what she'd been up to lately.

The last Thursday in April was a dreary, gray day. He felt particularly lonely and more than a bit put out at the idea of Kelly seeing someone, so he called her.

After a few minutes of chitchat, he got around to what was on his mind. "It really pisses me off when you tell me you're going out with a *friend*. I'm sure it's not a girl friend."

Kelly replied, "You know, Jake, being nice to you becomes more and more difficult."

"Okay, okay. Don't get upset. I'm just making conversation. Never mind. So, you said there was a problem about next weekend?"

"I have a cousin that's getting married in Iowa, so the children and I will be gone."

"Damn. I get to see them so seldom. On the other hand, if you're with the kids, I don't have to worry about you."

"Unlike you, I don't need looking after all the time. Get my point, Sherman?" she shot back.

He thought, She's got me there. He glanced at his casts. "Well, have a good time. I gotta get back to work. Bye." He fumbled and nearly dropped the receiver as he hung up. What a fucking hassle these casts were.

He went over to the bar and told George to pour him a drink. One of the customers looked at him and asked, "How do you get by with a cast on each hand?"

"How the hell do you think I get by? Not easily!" Jake roared.

"I bet it's hard even scratching your balls," the customer grinned.

"How about if I take this cast and shove it up your ass?"

The customer put his hands up. "Testy, testy." He got off his stool and went to the other end of the bar, away from Jake.

Jake looked at George. "Everyone around here thinks they're a fucking comedian." He sighed. "George, I'm sick of this conversation. Let's change the subject. Did you ever read the book about Jekyll and Hyde?"

"Who and who?"

"You know, Jekyll and Hyde. The doctor that turns into a monster."

"Jake, how many drinks have you had tonight?"

"Obviously not enough, so start bringing me doubles," he grumbled.

Jake surveyed the bar. He found himself hoping for a reason to smack someone tonight. By the time he finished a few more drinks, his anger had only increased. He was itching for a fight.

A disturbance caught his attention.

"Hey, bartender, you shortchanged me!" a customer yelled at George.

"Aha!" Jake said gleefully under his breath, and hustled over.

With the cast on his right arm, he backhanded the customer across the bridge of his nose and knocked him off his stool.

Then he kicked him two or three times. "Still think you've been shortchanged, jerkoff?" Jake said, looming over the man writhing in pain on the floor.

"You broke my nose," the man cried. "You broke my nose!"

George leaned over the bar and looked at the guy, and laughed. "Kick him once for me, but don't touch his sore nose!" he told Jake.

"Okay," Jake answered cheerfully, then kicked the guy three more times, happy to take out his frustration on someone who he thought deserved it. A couple more kicks for good measure, and Jake was done. He felt a lot better.

Jake extended his arms for everyone to see and announced, "Now, there's no way I'm picking this asshole up and hauling him outta here with these casts. So someone else needs to—or he'll just lie here."

A couple of regulars chuckled and stepped up. "This should entitle us to free drinks!"

A few minutes later, Jake was surprised to see the guy that he had beaten up walk back in the Poodle, accompanied by two beat cops he recognized.

"Hey, Jake, can we see you in the cloakroom?" one of the cops asked.

Curious, Jake followed the three men. When the four of them were alone, the cops grabbed a hold of the guy's arms.

"Mr. Sherman," one of the uniformed officers stated, "this individual said you beat him up for no reason."

As he said this, the other officer punched the guy in the stomach.

Jake was shocked but held his tongue.

The second policeman asked the poor bastard, who was wide-eyed and groaning, "Did you want to press charges?" and punched him in the gut again.

The guy hunched over in pain and mumbled something.

"Speak up. I can't hear you," the first cop said. He accompanied his order with yet another punch.

"No!" the guy moaned loudly, trying to break free.

The cops winked at Jake and dragged the guy, half stumbling, out the front door.

On his way home that night, somewhat more sober, he thought about the poor schmuck he and the cops had beaten up. He'd definitely overreacted . . . and so had the police. It reminded him of his Jekyll and Hyde dream and that still replayed in his head nearly every time he had to get physical with someone. Could that scenario be his future? 'Nice guy goes bad?' Because that was definitely Mr. Hyde who beat up that customer tonight.

"I have got to get that book to see how it ends," he muttered, "and the sooner the better."

THE NEXT NIGHT WAS FRIDAY, and Frank was the bouncer. When Jake saw him, he had Frank join him at a quiet table in the corner while he related the story of how he and the cops had beaten up the poor SOB the night before. He wondered what Frank's reaction would be.

Frank said, "I appreciate your concern, Jake, but I don't really want to hear this. Sometimes, shit just happens." He stood up.

Jake leaned back in his chair. "Yeah, okay, I hear ya, but . . . " He wasn't done yet. "You know, it kinda reminded me of a picture I saw in the paper recently with an article on the 1968 Democratic Convention in Chicago. The photograph was of a policeman clubbing a helpless woman. Now that's an example of police brutality, wouldn't you say?"

McPherson laughed and shook his head. "Jake, what the picture didn't show—and the article didn't say—was that the woman was in the process of biting the cop's thumb off! Now, what would you have done?"

"I'd have shot the bitch!"

"Exactly," Frank said and walked away.

This information made a stunning impression on Jake. Not all policemen were bad guys, despite what he'd witnessed last night. He'd been raised to believe they were all pigs. But he counted Frank as a good guy, as were many of the cops who came into the Poodle for a drink now and then. The cops from last night might have had more information about the guy they'd all beaten up than Jake had—just like the situation in the news photo. Jake needed to trust the cops more.

It was time, he thought, to revise his old belief about the police, and especially about violence in general. Violence was okay—even necessary—in certain situations, especially at the Poodle, he rationalized.

JAKE USUALLY SPENT HIS SATURDAY NIGHT off with the kids, but since they and Kelly were out of town, he decided to go bar hopping instead. He knew all the bartenders so, at each place, he bought a drink and then the house bought him one or two. Jake left big tips and everyone was happy.

By the time he arrived at the Blue Ox, he was more than half in the bag. He waved at George's girlfriend, Joyce, across the room, and then sat down at the bar next to a good-looking blonde. He said to her, "I'll let you buy me a drink, but don't think I'm easy. It would take several to get me into bed with you." She didn't seem amused, so Jake craned his neck to see if there was anyone else in the place he could hustle. Since there were no other likely candidates, he got off his stool and went to take a leak instead.

Without getting his casts wet, he rinsed his face as best he could. "I'm not losing my touch, am I?" he muttered to his reflection in the mirror. *Nah.*

He headed back to his stool and the blonde. He faced her and said, "Okay, you talked me into it."

She turned her face away and said to the guy on the other side of her, "See what I mean?"

A second later, something hit him on the side of his head and, as he was falling, that something hit him again. Sprawled on the floor, he slipped in and out of consciousness but was aware of someone punching him from above. Suddenly the beating stopped.

"Bring me a cold rag," a voice boomed, then said to him, "Easy, Jake, don't try to get up. You've got a nasty cut above your ear and, boyo, you're going to have one hell of shiner in the morning."

"What the hell happened?" Jake mumbled.

"Some unfortunate sucker punched you, Jake, and now he's on his way to the hospital. I stopped him before he could do any more damage."

The other voice sounded familiar. "Andy, is that you?"

"Yeah, it's me, your ex-brother-in-law."

Andy Hurley was Kelly's younger brother. At over six feet and more than two hundred pounds, he'd played hockey in school and had a reputation of being a vicious street fighter.

"Thanks for saving my ass. I really appreciate it," Jake said as he sat up.

"Don't think anything about it," Andy replied, helping Jake stand and lean against the bar. "You got me out of some jams when I was a kid on more than one occasion. Now, let me help you to your car."

Jake put his arm around Andy's neck and, grinning, said, "The night is young and we're going to get very drunk!"

JAKE SOMEHOW MANAGED TO GET HOME and immediately fell unconscious into bed.

Jake's mother leaned out the window from their apartment on the second floor in the four-flat they lived in and called out, "Jacob, Jacob! It's time for supper. Go get your brother."

Jake was playing tag football in the street and tried to ignore her but soon gave up. "Ma, he'll be home. We're in the middle of a game here."

She yelled, "Damn it, go right now!"

Reluctantly Jake left his friends and walked the block and a half to the pool hall. He knew where to find his fifteen-year-old brother because Larry hung out there all the time.

At nine years old, Jake didn't like going into the pool hall. The people scared him and the place stunk of cigarette smoke. Jake paused, took a deep breath, and walked inside.

Much to his surprise, it wasn't the pool hall. It was a saloon, just like in the movies. A piano played. There were cowboys with spurs and cowboy hats, and lots of women showing plenty of skin. Everyone was drinking and smoking and all of the cowboys wore guns. Two of the men were pushing Larry around.

Jake was furious. Not for the first time, he felt protective of his older brother. "Stop!" he yelled.

All heads turned toward Jake.

"Kill that little fucker!" someone yelled.

Several of them drew their guns and Jake thought he recognized one of them as Lucky Doyle. Same dark, cold, empty eyes.

Jake instinctively reached down with both hands and, much to his surprise, discovered that he had guns holstered on each hip, just like the men in the saloon. Unfortunately, because of the casts, he couldn't draw his weapons. He couldn't defend himself. He was screwed.

He stood there, frozen, a target. The Doyle look-alike fired several shots into him. It hurt like hell—like a hot poker jabbing him repeatedly in the gut. He put his hands on his stomach to stop the blood from pouring out of him.

I'm going to die.

Just before he keeled over, he said, "My mother is going to be really mad at me." He was dead before he hit the floor.

He awakened to a loud banging on his bedroom door.

His roommate, Pete, called through the door, "Jake? Are you all right?"

He struggled to catch his breath and sat up, groggy. He looked down and discovered there was no blood and no bullet holes. Just his damp sheets twisted around him. He was surprised to be unhurt. The dream had seemed so real.

"I'm okay. Thanks, Pete. Just a bad dream."

He looked at his casts. He couldn't wait to get these fucking things off.

The nightmare had been a doozy. He wondered what it had meant. "It's got to be about the Poodle and that fucking thorn in my side, Doyle. I can't believe what that place is doing to me. I've *got* to find another job."

This wasn't the first time he'd said that, he realized, and it was becoming his new mantra. Maybe someday he'd actually do it.

JAKE FINALLY GOT AROUND TO BUYING the Jekyll and Hyde book. He read a couple of chapters each day before he went to work. Intrigued with the character's gradual transformation from Jekyll to Hyde, he wondered if that were really possible.

His fascination with the book soon became an obsession. Every time he had a confrontation at the Poodle with a customer, he thought about it afterward. "Maybe people really do transform from the good Dr. Jekyll into the vicious killer, Mr. Hyde." He wondered if Doyle had always been so evil, or if he had started off normal, too, like Jake and everyone else.

He tried to talk to George about it, because there was no one else who would possibly understand. "George, do you believe it's possible for people to unknowingly transform from their normal selves into something terrible and rotten to the core?"

George raised his eyebrows. The toothpick bobbed up and down one time. "Maybe it's time to switch your drinks, Jake." He added, "You haven't been taking drugs, have you?"

Jake sighed, frustrated. There was no one to share these misgivings with. He toyed with talking to Kelly about it but didn't want to scare her. Chances were, she would think he had really gone off the deep end.

"Maybe I have?" he asked himself.

On a warm May afternoon, Jake walked into the Poodle and showed off his left hand, now minus its cast. A doctor had removed it earlier that day.

"One down, one to go," he announced, delighted.

Jake still had a problem. The shoulder holster was under his left armpit, yet he needed his right hand—still in its cast—to unholster the gun.

Consequently, he had purchased a holster that rode under his right arm—not that he felt confident about drawing his gun with his left hand . . . but it was better than nothing. At least he could carry his gun again.

"Drinks on the house!" he said to everyone, then laughed and added, "Like hell, you fuckers! I'm the only one drinking on the house."

Laughter chimed in with a few boos, but he just ignored them all and went over to the bar to light up a cigarette and enjoy a celebratory Beam and soda in honor of one less cast.

CHAPTER 10

Sunday, May 13

JAKE PROPPED HIMSELF UP ON ONE ELBOW in Kelly's bed and said, "I have a story which I think is very funny, but I'm not sure you would think so."

Kelly sat up. "Okay, Jake, you've got me curious, so tell me, and I'll decide."

Reluctantly, because telling her this story was a bit iffy after all, he began. "You remember Kathy Arnold? She used to be married to Jack Greenbaum?"

"Yes, sure."

"Anyway, I've taken her out a couple of times, and as she's going down on me, she says, 'If Kelly doesn't want it anymore, I guess I'll take it now.'"

She punched him in the shoulder. Twice.

"Ouch! That hurts! Well, you had to be there."

She punched him again. "That's a disgusting story, but, at least she has good taste," Kelly said, bursting out laughing. Then they both lost it, laughing so hard that tears rolled down their cheeks.

JAKE WAS ENJOYING A QUIET NIGHT at work when in walked his nemesis, Doyle, with what appeared to be a young woman from the asshole's stable of prostitutes. Jake tried to take George's advice and stay as far away as possible, but he kept a sharp eye on Doyle.

A few minutes later, he saw Doyle slap the girl across the face. She cried out and nearly fell off her barstool.

Jake started to rush over but George got there first. He leaned over the bar and confronted Doyle. "Don't you ever fuckin' pull that shit around here again."

Doyle ignored George and looked at Jake approaching him. "I see you've got a gun, punk. I bet you wouldn't have the balls to use it."

Jake was infuriated and reached for his gun. Damn. He had the new holster on, with the gun under his right arm. He felt stupid as he fumbled while trying to get the gun out.

George immediately slid under the waitress station counter at that end of the bar and planted himself in between Jake and Doyle, his back to Jake. He growled to Doyle, "I also have a gun, mother fucker, and you know I'll use it."

Doyle looked between the two of them, sneered at Jake one more time, then grabbed the girl and said, "I've had enough of this fuckin' place." He stomped out, the sniffling girl in tow.

Jake gave up trying to get the gun out. It was way too late anyway.

Fucking cast. He had looked like an inept schmuck in front of Doyle just now.

THE NEXT NIGHT, JAKE AND GEORGE had breakfast at Jimmy's Broiler.

"George, did the previous managers at the Poodle have as much trouble with Doyle as I seem to be having?"

"As a matter of fact," George grinned, "No, they did not. Doyle seems to have a hard on only for you."

"Huh," Jake grunted, remembering that Pat had said the same thing. It was time to change the subject before he got all worked up again about Doyle. "So, George, what did you guys do before I came along? Every so often someone will ask me about a former manager of the Poodle, and I don't have a clue."

George thought for a minute. "The last two were D-horns. They did drugs, booze, and sometimes didn't show up for work or call in. The last decent guy we had before you was Mike Hamel. He had a crazy streak like you, but he was bigger and stronger."

Jake poured them both another cup of coffee from the pot the waitress had left on the table. "So, what happened to him?"

"One night, we were both fighting at the same time, and I couldn't cover his back. Anyway, some prick hit him on the head with a beer bottle and gave him a concussion."

Jake leaned forward, expecting George to finish the story, but George picked up his fork and leisurely started eating again. Hell, Jake thought, the bastard did it to me again. He hated it when he did that. "Well, don't leave me hanging, then what the fuck happened?"

"What the fuck do you think happened? He ended up in the hospital for two weeks. He never came back to work and the last time I saw him, he acted like he had taken one too many punches."

Jake toyed with his empty coffee cup and mulled over what George had told him, wondering if he would suffer a similar fate.

As they were leaving the restaurant, George turned to Jake and said, "On second thought, Mike Hamel wasn't as crazy as you are!"

JAKE WENT HOME AND DECIDED TO try out the gun with his left hand. It was about 3 a.m. so no one was around to bother him. He aimed the gun at a tree in the back yard, about twenty-five feet away.

"Oh shit, what if I miss the tree and hit someone next door?"

He walked closer to the tree and pretended it was Doyle. From about ten feet away, he fired a couple of shots. He hit the tree both times.

The shots echoed and the loud noise surprised him. He hustled into the house before someone called the cops.

JAKE HATED SUNDAYS. GEORGE WAS OFF, and at the first sign of trouble, the part-time bartender, Nick Stephano, would disappear.

One Sunday in May, Jake went about his daily tasks: he counted and delivered the till, and checked the dining room to make sure the tables were set and ready to go. He spoke to the cook and wait staff. He asked Nick if he needed more booze, and he went down-stairs to the liquor room and brought up the needed bottles. When he came up, he noticed two things.

First, Jose Johnson had arrived and was seated at the far end of the bar next to the waitress station. Second, four young black guys in their early twenties were standing at the bar, sucking up their drinks. Jake wondered if Nick had checked their IDs. The newcomers were pretty loud, and he would have to keep a close eye on them.

Sure enough, a few minutes later one of the wait staff complained to Jake that they were talking shit to her, including asking for a blow job for the four of them. This was exactly what Jake feared. He went to the office to retrieve his club, which he jammed in the back waistband of his pants. He pulled the gun out of its holster, checked to make sure the safety was off, and re-holstered it.

He approached the group. "Fellas, you have to leave."

One of them said, "Hey, mother fucker! You gonna make us?"

Another one added, "You don't look like shit to me, man."

As they tried to surround Jake, he backed up a few feet so that his back was against the wall. The situation was escalating and Jake looked to Nick to at least call the cops. As usual, when trouble came calling, Nick was nowhere to be found.

Jake was scared shitless. *Mr. Hyde, if you're in there, come on out.*

A burst of energy shot through him, and Jake knew what he had to do. He reached for the club with his good hand. Suddenly Jose Johnson loudly cleared his throat in the now silent room.

"Hey, you niggers," he called from his seat at the bar. "Number one, Mistuh Sherman gonna kill ya, and number two, if he don't, I *for sure* am gonna kill you!" Jose stood up and started to reach for his gun.

The four guys ran out of the bar.

Jake let out a huge sigh of relief. He realized he'd been holding his breath. His hands trembled, and he wiped his brow with the arm of his sport coat. Fuck, that was a close one.

He gathered himself, and felt weak in the knees as he staggered over to Jose. "I can't begin to thank you. But, tell me, why would you want to help?"

In his gravelly voice that was hard to understand, Jose replied, "Well, when you first started workin' here, you gave me a ration of shit for selling stuff in the bar. I thought, just another bigot pickin' on the niggers. But after watchin' you for a few months, I realized, man, that you treat everyone the same. Black or white. So you okay in my book."

Jake acknowledged the compliment and went behind the bar to get a drink for Jose and himself. Nick suddenly reappeared.

"Where the fuck have you been, you worthless piece of shit!" Jake demanded, giving free rein to his temper.

Nick held out his arms wide. "Mr. Sherman, fighting isn't in my job description."

JAKE FINALLY HAD THE SECOND CAST removed. That day at work, he said to George, "I feel like celebrating, plus, it's nearly June—that time of the year when I switch drinks."

"I could ask you why, but I really don't care. So what's it going to be?"

"It's going to be a gin and tonic, my good man," he said in an exaggerated British accent. "And don't forget the lime."

"Whatever," George muttered.

IT WAS SATURDAY NIGHT, AND THE place was busy. Frank was working as a bouncer. He came up to Jake and said quietly, "Jake, there's a card game tonight with a few of the guys, a few cops. You probably know some of them. It's an honest game; they're good guys, no hassles."

Jake hesitated. He wasn't into playing cards very much, but, what the hell, it was something to do. "What are the stakes?"

"Oh, you know, a buck ante. A limit on the raises of three bucks. You could lose—at the most—a hundred or so."

"Where is it at?"

Frank gave him the St. Paul address.

Jake pondered the invitation. Kelly's attitude had been less than amorous lately, so he might as well go. He and Frank agreed he'd follow Frank over there in his own car.

Jake was one of the last to leave the poker game at about 4 am. He was disgusted with himself for playing. It wasn't because he lost; he actually won sixty bucks. No, the problem was that he drank too much and the booze was awful. He knew he would pay dearly for it the rest of the day. He already felt like shit and it would only get worse.

He got in his car and began the long drive home. "Have to be careful not to get pulled over," he reminded himself.

He had driven a few blocks when he spotted a dark-colored nondescript car up on the curb with the motor running. His first instinct was to keep going. Tough shit for the slob in the car.

He had enough problems of his own . . . but what if the guy had had a heart attack or something? Oh shit, he'd better have a look. He pulled over and got out.

He opened the car's door on the driver's side and, much to his surprise, saw Frank MacPherson slumped over the steering wheel, snoring away. He reeked of booze.

"Frank, Frank," Jake said as he shook him. "Wake up. Wake up, buddy."

Frank muttered something and put his head back down on the steering wheel.

Jake shook him again. "Listen to me, MacPherson. Wake the fuck up before a squad car shows up."

That seemed to get through to him.

Frank blinked a few times opened his eyes. Slurring his words, he said, "Shit. Me, a Minneapolis cop, getting caught here in St. Paul. They'd fry my ass, and it could mean my badge."

Jake helped Frank into the Mustang, went back to Frank's car, backed it onto the edge of the street, and then he parked and locked it. When he got back into his own car, he said, "Okay, let's find a place that's open and we'll get some coffee into you."

They went to Mickey's Diner, a landmark that been around forever. Jake and Frank drank coffee, smoked cigarettes, and eventually sobered up—somewhat.

Jake drove Frank home, then headed to his own place in Wayzata, arriving just in time to see Pete leaving for work. Jake set the alarm for 2:30 pm and crashed.

When the alarm went off, Jake awoke in a rotten mood. His head pounded and his body ached. He'd have to have the Old Man give him a neck adjustment. He swore to himself for the thousandth time that he had to change his ways.

CHAPTER 11

Friday, June 1

THE LEGISLATORS, IN ALL THEIR WISDOM, had lowered the drinking age to eighteen, effective June first. To Jake, that meant more headaches. He talked to Pat about hiring some young waitresses to help deal with the younger crowd he expected would find their way to the Poodle. Pat agreed so Jake placed an ad in the *Minneapolis Tribune*.

He interviewed a few candidates and hired two girls. Sasha and Dawn.

Sasha Debrovner spoke with an accent he couldn't place, probably Eastern Europe. She was about Jake's height and built like Jayne Mansfield through the chest. She talked like she knew the score. He thought that she would have no trouble taking care of herself.

Dawn Pilger, on the other hand, was as wholesome-looking as they came. She was slender and of average height. Her light brown hair fell in waves midway down her back. She looked very innocent and naïve—like someone's teenage daughter. Jake questioned himself as to why he would hire someone so young looking, and he decided the contrast between her and Mansfield would be an excellent combination for the customers. They could have their pick: Jayne Mansfield fantasies, or dreams about the sweet, girl-next-door, Sally Field type. He had his bases covered.

Dawn's father came to see Jake the night before she started.

"Mr. Sherman, I'm concerned about my daughter's safety in a place like this—no offense," Mr. Pilger said.

Jake shook his hand and assured him, "I'll watch out for her like she was my own daughter, Mr. Pilger."

The father left and Jake thought, Why did I make such a stupid statement?

He didn't ask George what he thought, but George offered his opinion anyway. "The broad with the big knockers is okay, but the little one won't last a week."

Jake jumped all over that remark. "That's what you said about me and, lo and behold, I'm still here, Georgie!"

He often tried to impress his friends by coming up with a classic line from a movie to fit the moment, but it had become obvious that George didn't go to movies. Not that Jake went very often anymore either, since he worked nights, but still. It was discouraging when his witty quotes fell on deaf ears.

Jake was of two minds about how the lower drinking age would affect life at the Poodle. He planned for the worst because mixing the young crowd with the older inmates could be a problem. But he hoped for the best—that the two groups would mesh and the Poodle would have more business.

THE EIGHTEEN-YEAR-OLD DRINKING LAW had been in effect for two weeks and so far there weren't too many problems.

Sasha became an instant hit. The men ogled her and she handled it in a smart-mouth type of way that appealed to Jake. She gave as good as she got. Because of her large breasts, the nickname Jake had given her, Mansfield, had stuck. It worked.

Dawn, on the other hand, was too quiet. The bar crowd liked her but Jake had some concerns. She was too gullible and susceptible to some of the wise guys that hung out there.

One of the wise guys was Lucky Doyle. He was especially charming to Dawn—certainly out of character for Doyle. Jake was sure he had an ulterior motive. For one thing, he actually tipped her, which was unusual for the scumbag that Jake knew him to be.

Jake decided he'd have to sit down with Dawn and have a heart-to-heart with her about Doyle. After all, he'd made a promise to the girl's father. And besides, she was a sweet kid who didn't deserve to get sucked into Doyle's world. Jake began to regret hiring her.

EVEN WITH HIRING THE TWO NEW GIRLS, the Poodle didn't attract many of the young crowd. Nor did the law change bring trouble, much to Jake's relief.

Until tonight, that was. Trouble walked in the door at about eight o'clock. At well over six feet tall, the solidly built young man looked like he could play either NBA basketball or pro football. And considering the guy was dressed like a lumberjack in a flannel shirt, Jake leaned more toward Paul Bunyan. The kid's face, however, looked like that of a sixteen-year-old.

George checked his ID and served him. When the kid started on his third drink, he suddenly began pounding his fist on the bar and howling like a wolf.

Jake and George made eye contact. George rolled his eyes. Oh shit, Jake thought, we have a major problem here.

Jake approached the young man and asked him to leave. To Jake's surprise, he stopped howling, got up from the bar stool, and, without comment, started walking towards the front door.

So far, so good, Jake thought with relief. Until the kid reached the foyer.

He turned and began swinging his arms and once again baying like a wolf. Because of where he stood, nobody could come in or out of the place. George came out from under the bar, and he and Jake had a quick meeting.

Jake said, "Let's call the cops and they can handle it."

"Nah, we can handle this by ourselves. No need to call them."

Jake concurred because every time the police came, it was recorded, and too many calls could jeopardize the liquor license.

But he still thought they were going to need some additional help. Lenny wasn't around that night, so he called to Jimmy Box and another hood, Doug Gleason, who sat on their usual bar stools. "Hey, Jimmy, Doug. We need your help!"

Jake and George tried to distract the giant with conversation, while directing Jimmy and Doug to each grab one of his arms. They tried to drag him out the door but the kid was like an immovable rock.

George looked at Jake and shrugged, then punched the kid with several solid blows. Paul Bunyan finally stopped baying, at least, but that was the only recognition he gave that anything unusual was happening. He still wouldn't budge.

George stepped aside, and Jake hit him with his club. Then it was George's turn, then Jake's. Then George's again, then Jake's. The kid continued to stare straight ahead, and didn't try to shake loose from Jimmy and Doug's grip, nor did he ever flinch.

While George took his turn pounding on the kid, Jake watched the mesmerized bar crowd laugh and take bets as to who would tire first—George, Jake, or the kid. The kid still looked impervious to the beating he was taking.

After a couple minutes, Jake yelled to George, "His knees are starting to bend!"

They continued to hit him and finally he went down. It took the four of them to drag the guy out of the bar and throw him on the sidewalk. Surprisingly, he didn't look that much worse for wear. He was bleeding from his nose and mouth, but still appeared conscious. The young man groaned and said, "Whaddya do that for?"

Jake looked down at him and said, "And how did you enjoy the play, Mrs. Lincoln?"

Back inside things settled down, and Jake and George laughed, thinking the whole situation was pretty funny, now that it was over.

Jake wondered if there was a full moon tonight. That would explain the baying, Jake snickered to himself. It certainly didn't explain how that guy could take so many blows, however. The vision of a werewolf crossed his mind, and Jake laughed even harder. Nope, not a werewolf. Definitely more of a Frankenstein type and probably on drugs.

He thanked Jimmy and Doug for their help, bought them each a drink, and announced to everyone in the bar, "I expect to receive a cut from those of you that bet on me and George."

That brought more laughter. The regulars slapped him on the back, but nobody coughed up any money.

The Paul Bunyan story lasted the rest of the night. It became an inspiration for lots of jokes, good and bad. By the end of the evening, Jake figured he'd gotten all he could out of the poor slob's plight.

Another job well done, Jake decided. And he was going to celebrate. Still feeling psyched, and with a pleasant buzz from the drinks he'd tossed back, he scanned the room to find a doll to celebrate with.

JAKE AWOKE WITH THE FEELING THAT someone had just stabbed him in the eye. He needed to piss or his bladder would explode, and he would die right then and there. Not knowing where he was or how he got there, he just needed to find a bathroom.

It was so pitch black that Jake had no idea how he was going to find the damn can. He got up and staggered until he ran into a wall. Then, feeling his way, he moved slowly until his hand found an opening.

He entered and suddenly he was attacked by something scratching, clawing at him. Jake swung wildly at the monster, throwing lefts and rights until he was exhausted and fell down.

The lights came on and a naked girl said, "It's four a.m. What the fuck is the matter with you?"

Jake looked around and discovered that he had just had a fight with metal hangers in the closet.

And lost.

GETTING READY FOR WORK THE NEXT day, Jake looked in the mirror and saw how scratched up he was. What was he doing with his life? How did it get to be so shitty? How long was God going to punish him? And why couldn't He pick on someone else?

Jake smiled. It's payback for all your sins and transgressions, he told his reflection.

He continued to argue with himself. Okay, so he could've been a better husband and father. He could've been a better son, better student, better—oh, fuck it! He could stop feeling sorry for himself and get his ass to work.

He climbed into his Mustang and backed out of the driveway. He turned on the air conditioning because it was so damn hot outside, but nothing happened.

"Shit."

He'd forgotten the AC was on the fritz. He began to sweat, so he rolled down the windows, but that didn't help until he got on to Wayzata Boulevard and picked up enough speed to create a breeze through the car.

His thoughts shifted to the day ahead. Managing the Poodle gave Jake a unique opportunity to observe all kinds of people. Someday he'd have to write a book about his experiences here. Would anybody think the story was plausible? Not a chance. Even he could hardly believe it.

Jake went about his normal duties, and by eight p.m., he had assumed his regular position, leaning against the bar. Without asking, George put a drink down in front of him—a gin and tonic, with a twist of lime. He picked up the chilled glass.

"Put it down, you sonofabitch!" a waitress yelled from the dining room. "You took that money from the table!"

Oh, fuck, a robbery!

George vaulted over the bar and told Jake, "Cover the back! I'll go to the front."

Yanking his piece out of the shoulder holster as he ran to the back entrance of the dining room, he thought, Oh my God, I may really have to use this gun.

He rounded a corner and found himself staring into the face of a panicked-looking young man. In addition to stealing the money, the kid had also picked up a steak knife and, wild-eyed, he brandished it nervously, with the business end of it pointed at Jake.

Jake aimed his gun at the kid's chest and said slowly, "Put down the knife. If you haven't done it by the count of five, then when I'm finished, I will put a hole in you."

The kid turned a paler shade of white.

"One . . . two—"

"Shoot him! Shoot him!" Old Man Blumenthal yelled from behind Jake.

Christ, thought Jake, that's all we need right now, is this crazy old man egging me on. He refocused on the kid. "... three ..."

"... four ..."

The kid threw the knife down and raised his hands in surrender. "Can-can I just give you the money back?"

Jake nodded. The kid hurriedly reached into his jeans pocket and held out a wad of bills. Jake grabbed it from him. "Now get the fuck out of here." The kid bolted and headed toward the door. That, and getting the money back, satisfied Jake.

"Why'd you let him get away? You should have shot him!" Blumenthal said.

"You want someone shot, you shoot him."

The Old Man just shrugged his stocky shoulders.

Jake strode past him and went back to the bar, thinking the situation had been resolved.

Out of the corner of his eye, Jake saw the Old Man come out of the office with a piece, then hot-foot it out the front door.

What the fuck was Carl doing with a gun?

George yelled to Jake, "You better go after him before he shoots himself."

Jake ran out just in time to see Carl fire the weapon. Twice.

Carl said, out of breath, "I think I got him. I think I got him!"

Jake looked down the brightly lit street. Hennepin Avenue was crowded with people this time of the evening, but he didn't see the kid. No harm, no foul. No one was lying on the sidewalk, bleeding—or even taking notice of them, for that matter.

But the Old Man is really off his track, Jake thought, somewhat surprised, as he turned back to Carl.

He took the gun and walked the excited old fart back inside. "I know you don't drink but ... maybe you should have a belt before you go home. Maybe it'll settle you down." Carl ignored him.

Jake looked at George, rolled his eyes, and told the Dragon Lady to take the Old Man home.

He tucked the gun in the back waistband of his pants and went into the office to call Pat at home.

"We have a huge problem," he told the Old Man's son. "We can't have your father going around shooting people." Jake explained what had gone down. "I don't think he hit anyone, but we can't be sure."

To his surprise, Pat's response was a question. "What was the make of the gun?"

"A .22 pistol. Why are you asking?"

"We're in luck," Pat said. "It's a throwaway piece, not registered to anyone. Just make sure to wipe it down and throw it in a dumpster on your way home tonight."

Jake hung up the phone and decided he needed to rethink his opinion of these two guys, father and son. The whole thing was too casual—Carl racing for a gun and finding one, and Pat's reaction, or lack of. What kind of people was he working for, really?

Besides, now it was on him to get rid of the thing. What if he got stopped by the police on the way home with it still in his possession? Pissed off that he had to clean up everyone's messes, Jake stayed in a bad mood the rest of the evening. Even a couple extra drinks didn't improve things.

Closing time finally arrived. Jake left the Poodle and drove up and down several alleys until he felt that no one was looking, then he threw the gun out the window of his Mustang and into a dumpster. He recalled what he'd been thinking earlier in the day when he drove to work—that maybe he should write a book someday. But like I said, he scoffed, who would believe me?

The next day when Jake arrived at work, Pat told him that one of the Old Man's bullets had grazed a pedestrian on the corner. Not a serious injury.

Jake was relieved that nobody was hurt—really hurt. The story circulated throughout the bar and became a standing joke among the customers. Don't fuck with Old Man Blumenthal and if you do, be sure and stand directly in front of him.

A few days later, about the same time of night, Jake was doing his thing, going up and down the bar to talk with customers, listening to their stupid jokes. He was still sober, having had only a couple of gin and tonics.

Jake watched everybody who entered the bar. Two guys came in and they looked familiar—maybe from the old neighborhood—but he couldn't place them. They were dressed in sport coats and slacks, nothing out of the ordinary. But they looked out of place in the Poodle. They were more the types to frequent Duffy's Bar about three blocks away. More upscale than the Poodle.

They spoke to one of the waitresses and she pointed toward Jake. The men approached.

"What can I do for you?" Jake asked.

They introduced themselves as Ken Desnick and Morty Rosen.

"Jake Sherman," he said, shaking their hands. "You're both from north Minneapolis, aren't you?"

They nodded.

He continued, smiling, because he'd been correct. "So what can I do for you?"

A look passed between the two men. Jake sensed a problem, and it put him on his guard.

Rosen said, "We play cards with your brother Larry, and he's written some bad checks."

Jake tensed up but tried to appear casual.

Shrugging, he replied, "I think that, if I were you, I wouldn't play cards with him anymore. Now, is there anything else?"

Desnick took a step forward and got too much into Jake's personal space, which was a big mistake as far as Jake was concerned. Desnick said, "Somebody's got to make the checks good or your brother might . . . get hurt."

Jake's temper flared, but he reined it in and forced himself to smile. "Let me see the checks."

Rosen gave them to him and, without looking at the checks, Jake tore them up into several pieces.

The bits of paper floated to the floor.

The looks on their faces were priceless.

Before they could respond, Jake pulled open his sport coat so they could see his .357 magnum. "Now listen very carefully, assholes, because I will only say it one time. First of all, you shouldn't let him play, because he's a loser and he has no money. Second, and most important, if anything happens to Larry, I will kill both of you. Now turn the fuck around and get the hell out of here before I decide to do it now."

Desnick and Rosen hustled out of the Poodle without saying another word.

Jake went over to the bar and asked for another drink.

George brought him one. "What was the deal with them? Problem?"

"No problem, George. Just another night at the asylum."

George shook his head. He wiped off the bar with a white towel and headed off to serve the next customer, leaving Jake to thoughts of his brother.

Larry was six years older, yet Jake thought of him as the younger brother—when he thought of him at all. They had never been close. Larry had gone into the navy for four years and Jake had left for the Marines a year before his brother got out, so they didn't see each other for five years. Growing up, Jake had had, on more than one occasion, to bail him out. Not surprising that he had to do it now.

He decided he would never confront Larry about this recent episode.

He's family, Jake thought, and I did the right thing.

JAKE FOUND HIMSELF ARRIVING AT THE POODLE earlier in the day as time went on. He didn't start work right away—he just hung out, had a free lunch, and shot the shit with the daytime customers. He didn't have anything else to do.

One weekday in late June, as luck would have it, Pat said to him as he walked in at about 11 a.m., "Boy, am I glad you showed up. I have no one to tend bar because the daytime bartender, John, called in sick. Can you help me out, Jake?"

Shit, he'd never tended bar before . . . but he did know how to drink.

"Sure, Pat, no problem," he replied, and got behind the bar. "Oh, I know people eat lunch in here, so who is going to take food orders? I can't do both."

Pat pointed at a waitress. "Betty does that. Don't worry."

He looked to see where various bottles of booze were kept, then cut up some lemons and limes. Within a couple of minutes, he noticed the stools were filling up quickly with the lunch crowd.

"All right, let me have your attention, guys," he announced to the room. "Today, there will be no fou-fou drinks!"

A few people asked why; others laughed. One guy yelled out, "What does that mean?"

"What it means," he said impatiently, "is that I'm not going to make a goddamned drink that requires a blender. The only kind of drink you can have today is a bourbon and soda, a scotch and soda, a rum and whatever. Is that clear enough?"

"Okay, okay," a few people muttered.

The customers fell into line and things started to flow. Even though it was a hassle—something he'd never done before and there was a lot of pressure on him to get through it—he did.

At one point, he tried to light up a cigarette, but he couldn't smoke it because he was too goddamned busy. Nor was there an opportunity to bullshit with the customers. It was all he could do to keep the drinks coming and survive until George turned up for his shift. Everyone watched him, waiting for him to fuck up, but other than that, the customers were supportive. Beyond a little kidding, no one hassled him.

On a few occasions, he poured the wrong drink and a customer called it to his attention. "Hey, that's not what I ordered."

"It is now!" Jake responded.

Finally, at a little before four, George walked in and took one look at him. "What the hell are you doing back there?"

"Don't worry, George, I'm not after your job. You can have it!"

They switched places and Jake went back out into the main area of the bar. He sat down on a stool, lit up a cigarette and took a deep drag. Ahh. He blew out the smoke. "George, pour me a drink." Dammit, he didn't care if it was only 4 p.m.—he'd earned it.

George pushed a gin and tonic across the bar at him. As he sipped it, he thought, "Every time I come in here early, there's a problem. I am fucking jinxed! Besides, I've been hanging out here too much lately. I'm starting to act like the customers, using the Poodle as my home away from home. From here on out, I'll arrive in time for my shift, and that's it."

CHAPTER 12

Wednesday, June 22

THREE WEEKS INTO THE NEW LAW allowing eighteen-year-olds to drink, the problems Jake thought would occur hadn't materialized.

One night after work, Jake and George had coffee at Jimmy's Broiler, and the conversation got around to the new law.

"I haven't noticed any significant increase in business, which is disappointing," George commented. "And on top of that, these young punks don't tip worth a damn."

Jake shrugged. "You can't win 'em all." George made most of his money off his tips—not his wages—so George got cranky when tips were bad.

Jake changed the subject and asked him what he thought about the two new waitresses and how they were doing.

"Mansfield is doing great. She takes orders properly and is good with the customers." George forked in a mouthful of hash browns, chewed and swallowed, then took a sip of coffee.

As George went for another mouthful of food, Jake said impatiently, "What do you think about Dawn? You haven't mentioned her."

"She's okay, but she's so fucking naïve. I don't know if you noticed, but Lucky Doyle came in a couple nights ago, and he seemed to have quite a conversation with her."

"Oh, that's not good," Jake said, leaning back in the booth. "Dammit, why did I promise her old man that I'd watch out for her?" He slammed his fist on the table, jarring the coffee cups. "I'd better talk to her tomorrow. She needs to stay away from that bastard."

"Just remember, Jake. He's a dangerous bastard."

THE NEXT EVENING, JAKE TOOK DAWN aside before she started her shift. He gave her the lowdown as to what kind of person Doyle was. "Here's some of the things we know he's done—he deals drugs, he's a pimp, and he's committed armed robbery. And there's probably a lot more that we don't know about."

Dawn's eyes widened. "But he seemed like such a nice man," she argued.

Jake lost his patience. "Stay away from him, Dawn. End of story." He ground out his cigarette and exited the office.

JAKE COULDN'T PUT THE SITUATION ABOUT Dawn and Doyle out of his mind. He had to do one of two things. Either deal with Doyle . . . or let Dawn go. The latter might be the best solution.

His thoughts were interrupted by one of the wait staff pointing out a lady at the bar who had had way too much to drink. Jake checked her out as he walked over to that section of the bar.

The middle-aged brunette woman was swearing up a blue streak and elbowing customers. By the time he got to her, she'd spilled her drink on the bar and the person next to her, who gave her a dirty look and moved out of her way. The loud-mouthed woman was Jake's height and must have weighed two hundred-plus pounds.

Jake tapped her on the shoulder to get her attention. "You've had enough to drink tonight, ma'am. We're not going to serve you anymore. I'll walk you out the front door."

She nodded and didn't say anything. Jake turned to walk toward the front door with her and—

Wham!

He went down for the first time in the Poodle.

Several stunned seconds later, he figured out she had decked him with her purse. She hadn't budged from her place at the bar, except to glare at him on the ground.

Laughing, George said, "I told you, if they act like a man, treat them like a man."

Jake picked himself up off the floor and took to heart what George had said.

He brought his arm back and punched her in the face.

The punch had its desired effect. She slid off the barstool and sat down on the floor with her purse still clutched in her fist.

His hands on his hips, Jake scowled down at her. "Here's what's going to happen. We're going to help you up and walk you out of the bar. And if you give me any lip, I'm really going to hurt you." She nodded shamefacedly.

George was still laughing when Jake came back into the bar.

"Go fuck yourself, George, and get me a drink."

A COUPLE OF DRINKS LATER, JAKE MADE the mistake of asking himself what else could go wrong tonight. There was a full moon, which usually meant that the crazies would be out in force. George told Jake to be on alert, "because we'll get our share of the fuckers," he explained.

Soon after that, Reggie called from the Hotel Anthony and said that someone had reported a lady on the third-floor fire escape. She was threatening to jump.

"What the fuck do you want me to do about it?" Jake retorted.

"Please, Jake. I need to stay at the front desk," Reggie pleaded.

"All right," Jake relented, not taking it too seriously but deciding to check it out. He walked next door, climbed the steps to the third floor, and opened the door at the end of the hallway that led to the black metal fire escape outside.

Jake did a double take. An extremely large, heavyset woman was leaning over the railing. She could have been a sister of the woman he had just thrown out of the Poodle.

She leaned over the railing and looked ready to jump. When she turned to stare at Jake, her eyes were empty of emotion. It was as if she was looking right through him.

"Come on, lady. Come back inside with me. You don't really want to do this."

She didn't move.

He tried several other things—he even offered her a drink on the house and to call someone for her if she would just come back inside—but she didn't respond to anything he said.

After ten minutes of cajoling, Jake was fed up. He made a quick calculation: If he went out there on the tiny landing and tried to physically wrest her back inside, and if she jumped then, she would no doubt take him with her.

Thinking he could defuse the tension, he tried another tactic. "If you're going to jump, do it now; I have to get back to work." She turned away from Jake and jumped.

He didn't fucking believe this! The lady had actually fucking jumped. Jesus!

He raced to the railing and looked over the edge. It was too dark to see anything, and the streetlights didn't penetrate the narrow gap between the two buildings.

He jogged back downstairs and told Reggie, "She jumped! Better call the cops and an ambulance."

He went back to work, had a few more bumps to calm down, and told George and several of the customers the story. They all had a big laugh but Jake was still a bit shook up.

Reggie told him later that she apparently bounced between the Hotel Anthony and the Poodle—which were only four feet apart—and that she broke her shoulder and had a few bruises. That was it.

On his way home that evening, he reflected on the two experiences with women. He decided that the place had made him so hard and callused that he had hit a woman, *and* had been willing to watch another one try to commit suicide. He really needed to have his head examined.

JAKE HAD THE WEEKEND OFF. KELLY had agreed to have a picnic with him and the children on Sunday. He cooled it on the drinking the night before so he would be fresh and could run around with the kids. They'd both spent the night at friends' houses on Saturday, so he didn't get to have them at his house. Having Kelly go with them to the river on a picnic—they would be a family again for the day—would more than make up for lost time with his kids.

He arrived at the house at ten-thirty, wearing shorts.

Kelly wore a creamy-colored sundress and looked especially beautiful. When she saw him ogling her, she said, "I know that look, Sherman! Just remember, this is a family outing and no hanky panky, agreed?"

Jake smiled—"Your wish is my command"—and gave an exaggerated bow.

The children hugged and kissed him. They were excited to see him and anxious to get started. "Where are we going, Fath?"

"To the St. Croix River!" he announced.

"Yay! Can we go swimming?" Sarah already had her one-piece bathing suit on, and Sean wore blue swimming trunks.

They loaded the car with fried chicken, potato salad, fruit, soft drinks, and brownies for dessert. Then they piled into the Mustang and off they went, heading east to the river, singing all the way.

During the drive, Jake thought about how he should have been doing much more of this family type of thing when he and Kelly were still married. He kept looking over at Kelly and, in the rearview mirror, at the children bouncing in the backseat. This is actually kinda fun, he thought.

After forty-five minutes of driving, they arrived. The kids bounded out of the car and Jake went after them because he didn't want them in the water by themselves. The kids swam, he waded in the river, and they all played catch on the sandy beach that they had to themselves. The temperature was seventy-five degrees and with a clear blue sky, it couldn't have been a more perfect day.

They played Frisbee, then tag. After they finished lunch, Jake said to the kids, "I'm pooped. You guys have run me ragged. I'm going to take a break." Sarah and Sean wandered off to chase butterflies.

He sat on the blanket next to Kelly. She was lying down, looking up at the sky.

"This is nice," she said and let out a big sigh.

Jake just looked at her for a few minutes, and drank in her beauty. He knew how the day could be even more perfect. "I'm going to break my promise."

JAKE SPENT THE NIGHT WITH KELLY. He woke the next morning, fixed breakfast for everyone, kissed Kelly and the kids good-bye, and headed home to get ready for work. Before he left, he told her he would stop at the hardware store to get the part to fix the toilet she'd been complaining about not working properly.

ON HIS WAY DOWNTOWN, HE THOUGHT about his life and his job at the Poodle.

He had been there for six months, and in many ways it had been six months too long. He knew he could do better than managing a joint full of dysfunctional people. He asked himself why he hadn't looked for another job yet.

You're stuck in a rut, he told himself.

No, he argued, I just don't want to leave badly enough to do anything about it. That's not procrastinating, he assured himself.

Maybe it was time to add up the pluses and minuses of working at The Poodle—maybe that would motivate him.

On the positive side, he made decent money. And he had taken control of the place, which enhanced his self-esteem.

On the negative side, he knew that he had changed his demeanor in order to fit in. He drank and swore more, and carried a gun. He had discovered a propensity for violence that had not previously existed. He'd been involved in more fights at the Poodle in six months than he had during the two years he'd spent in the Marine Corps, or, as a matter of fact, his whole life. His friends complained that they were having trouble relating to him, and none of them came around the Poodle. He missed them. And Kelly had recently started urging him to get a different job. Also, his increasing dislike of Doyle was rapidly becoming an obsession—no two ways about it.

Enough, asshole, he admonished himself. Quit feeling sorry for yourself. Get mentally ready for another fucking night in the jungle.

His thoughts turned back to Kelly. He tried not to think of her, but he was never successful for more than a few hours. He knew the mistakes he had made during their marriage. Behaving like a chauvinist pig was probably the biggest one. Men went to work and women stayed home and did all of the domestic chores–ha! What a jerk he'd been. He hit himself in the head with the palm of his hand.

Now, at least, when he went over to Kelly's, he did the wash, cut the grass, made small repairs, and, in general, anything that would make Kelly's life easier. She always thanked him, sometimes with an invitation to spend the night—but not nearly often enough for a chance at reconciliation, at least to Jake's way of thinking.

Bottom line, he had become more thoughtful when it came to the needs of his wife—ex-wife, he thought regretfully.

But it was all too little, too late.

He careened into a parking space, shifted his car into park, got out, and slammed the door. As he stalked into the Poodle, he only had one thing on his mind.

He needed a fucking drink!

CHAPTER 13

Thursday, July 5

S TEVE CANNON HAD STOPPED IN at the Poodle last night. Jake was pleased to see him. Steve was a well-known announcer for WCCO radio. He and Jake had met through a mutual friend, Will Shapira, right after Jake's divorce. They hit it off right away; they both had the same sense of humor. They'd played tennis several times the previous summer, went to a few bars together, and talked on the phone once or twice during the winter, but Jake hadn't seen him since before he'd started at the Poodle.

Steve didn't stay long because the Poodle wasn't his kind of place. Jake knew he preferred the more upscale bars.

Before he left, Steve told him about the movie *Deep Throat* and that he'd been wanting to see it, so he and Jake made arrangements to go the next day. Steve wasn't on the air until three, and Jake didn't need to be at the Poodle until his usual four.

The show started at 11 a.m. at the Rialto Theatre, located on Lake Street in a seedier part of town. There were only a dozen other people there.

The movie might've been the worst they had ever seen. It had been rated XXX and certainly lived up to expectations. Despite the poor acting, Jake and Steve laughed uproariously as they watched Linda Lovelace—frustrated that her hugely energetic sex life left her unsatisfied—seek medical help. They both laughed so hard,

Jake thought they were going to choke on their popcorn when the doctor informed Miss Lovelace that the reason for her problem was that her clitoris was mistakenly located at the back of her throat, and that there was a very simple remedy, which the doctor and various other men proceeded to demonstrate. Jake and Steve laughed until the tears rolled down their cheeks.

On the way out, Jake said, "I will never forget when she is sitting on the kitchen counter and that guy is going down on her, and she says, 'Do you mind if I smoke while you eat?'"

FEELING NO PAIN, JAKE LEANED ON THE BAR later that evening, waiting for another drink. He told everyone that listened about the movie and kept referring to the "Do you mind if I smoke while you eat?" comment. He got a good laugh from the crowd every time.

His thoughts turned to Kelly. He had just gotten off the telephone with her and had related the movie's punch line to her. She got a big kick out of it.

After he hung up, he tried to make sense of their situation. They had been divorced for a year and a half, and neither one seemed able to move on with their lives. He sighed and lit another cigarette. They didn't argue over the children, money, or anything in particular. He thought about their sex life. If he caught her in the right mood, he spent the night and shared her bed. The sex was good—no, it was great.

But *why* was it so great? Had she learned something from someone else? Once the thought lodged in his head, he couldn't shake it.

Aside from chuckling over the line from the movie, she had seemed distant tonight on the phone. Did she have a boyfriend? Was she sleeping with him? Jake couldn't stand to think about it—the idea of Kelly in someone else's bed gave him a headache.

"George, hit me again, and make it a double this time!"

George gave him the drink. "You keep this up and I'll have to carry you out of here."

Jake thought about saying something shitty but decided against it. Without George backing him up, he'd probably be in intensive care. George backed him up all the time—anytime there was a fight, Jake knew he could count on George's fists.

Nah, there was no point in pissing off George. He was the best friend Jake had at the moment. Damn near the only friend, Jake thought as he took a big swig of his gin and tonic, and knew once again he was wallowing in own bullshit.

He changed the subject and asked a question he'd been wondering about ever since he'd heard the rumor. "Do you really put your money under the dog house in your backyard?"

"You fucking better believe it," George grinned, the ever-present toothpick lodged between his teeth. "I don't trust the banks, and my eighty-pound German shepherd is all the security I need."

George smoothly poured a tall Budweiser from the tap for a customer, and just as smoothly slid it across the counter to him, laughing and chatting away with the growing crowd. Jake marveled at George's ability to do anything with a toothpick in his mouth—even fight. Jake had never quite got up the courage to ask him what he would do if someone hit him in the face and he ended up swallowing the damn thing.

Jake just shook his head and finished his gin and tonic. This place—and the people in it—were really bonkers.

JAKE WAS IN A VERY BAD mood. He had spent the last four nights with Kelly and he thought everything was going exceedingly well. It gave him hope that they really could get back together.

But as he dressed that morning, she dropped the bomb.

"This is it, Jake. I—we—have to move on with our lives, and it won't happen if we keep ending up in bed."

Jake froze in the act of pulling on his pants. Her comment shook him to his very core.

"What the hell brought this on?" he asked. "Is there someone else?"

"No. No, but I'm going to make a real effort to find someone else, and I suggest you do the same."

He finished dressing in a hurry, stormed out of the house, and didn't even say good-bye to the children. His mind raced as he drove home.

Why was this happening to him? Why did Kelly not want to get back together? He had thought they were making real progress. What could he do to change her mind?

At home, he stared blindly at the plain beige walls of his living room and tried to figure out whose fault this was.

That evening he went to work with a real chip on his shoulder. Nobody'd better fuck with me tonight, he thought as he stormed into the Poodle.

A few hours before closing and after Jake finished several drinks—he couldn't remember how many—he walked toward the back of the bar on his way to the can. One of the customers—someone Jake hadn't seen before—got off of his barstool and accidentally bumped into Jake.

"What did you say, asshole?" Jake roared. "You got a problem with me?"

Before the guy could respond, Jake hit him with a right and caught him solidly on the jaw. The guy fell backward, and Jake hit him two more times before he landed. Then Jake started kicking him.

"What the fuck are you doing?" George yelled. "Quit it, and get control of yourself."

Jake stopped. "What's wrong?"

George came around from behind the bar and helped the poor slob to his feet. He checked the guy out, decided there were no serious injuries, and told him, "You'll heal. Now leave."

George turned to Jake. "Let's go to the office, *now*. I want to talk to you in private, asshole."

Jake followed George to the back. What the fuck? Was he getting called to the principal's office, or what?

They went in the office and George slammed the door shut. "Jake, I gotta tell you, you've become a bigger pain in the ass than the customers. We're supposed to break up fights, not fucking start them," he growled, shaking his fist at Jake. "And another thing. You need to lighten up on the booze."

Angry and embarrassed, Jake turned and stalked out of the office without saying a word.

Yeah, okay, maybe he went too far. One kick would have been sufficient, Jake thought a few minutes later, when he was cooled down. George was right, though Jake certainly wasn't about to admit it.

Jake finished his shift without asking for another drink.

THE NEXT TIME JAKE HAD A DAY OFF, he went over to Kelly's and decided to tackle several little household chores and home repairs. He did the wash, fixed the gate, and cleaned out the gutters. Anything to get in her good graces, he thought. He also hoped Kelly would relent on her latest pronouncement about no sex.

When she got home, she admired his handiwork. "That's very nice, Jake. Thank you. But that doesn't change anything. Get it through your head: we are not an item anymore," she said gently, looking him straight in the eye.

Damn. She knew him too well. He sighed and went into the kitchen to make an afternoon snack for the kids. He wasn't giving up; he'd keep on truckin', as the saying went.

He tried to talk to her about it one more time before he left the house. "Why do you feel so strongly about—"

"I have told you," she interrupted him, "that we need to get on with our lives. You and I have no future, Jake."

He left the house, feeling more sad than he had in a long time. Driving to work, his anger and frustration grew. "What do I have to do to get back with my wife?" Then he remembered. "She's my *ex*-wife!" he yelled, pounding the steering wheel. *Fuck.*

Besides, how was he supposed to meet anyone? He worked at the damned Poodle.

CHAPTER 14

Monday, July 16

GOD WORKS IN MYSTERIOUS WAYS, JAKE thought a couple of nights later when he noticed a beautiful blonde walk into the Poodle. She had come in with another woman and they seemed to know the waitress, Cathy.

The woman's classy apparel made her seem out of place in the Poodle. She was probably just slumming, he decided. Nonetheless, it was worth a try, so he asked Cathy to introduce them. During the ensuing conversation, he learned that she was a stewardess for Braniff airlines.

She seemed more than a little interested. Jake talked to her off and on that night, when he had the chance. He discovered she was not only good-looking but intelligent too. He was thinking about his next move when she surprised him by asking him to stop over at her place after work.

He told her he wouldn't get out of the Poodle until two in the morning. She didn't blink.

Hot damn, he was going to get laid tonight. He all but rubbed his hands together in anticipation.

However, there was still the problem of where to screw her. He certainly was tempted to hightail it to Ms. Braniff's apartment the second he got off work, but he told her she would have to follow him back to his place . . . mentally keeping his fingers crossed.

"I would," she said, her face a picture of regret, "but I have an early flight tomorrow, and I need to be home."

He didn't think about it for long. "Okay, give me your address."

AN ALARM CLOCK BUZZED and he woke up. Looking at the girl lying next to him, who stretched and smiled coyly at him, he thought for a minute, then it came to him. *Bridget, yes, Bridget is her name.* He smiled back at her. This was progress. Usually he couldn't remember the broad's name.

"I would be willing to miss my flight today," she said, flirting with her eyes and her hands, "because I'm really enjoying this."

"Oh, you shouldn't miss your shift, Bridget," he said. He knew he sounded noble, but in reality, he was planning to spend most of the day with his children. And no matter how great the piece of ass, he made no exceptions to his time with his kids.

JAKE WAS IN A GOOD MOOD that night after hanging out all day with Sarah and Sean at their house. He hoped his good spirits would last. If he could just go one night without a fight, he might consider going back to the synagogue on a regular basis. Just kidding, he smiled to himself.

Sure enough, a little later some drunk threatened another customer. Jake rushed over and grabbed the drunk by his collar and belt, and led him to the front door. They'd nearly made it when Jake tripped over the drunken man's foot, and they both stumbled and fell.

Jake ended up on top of the man. "You fucking bum," Jake snarled. "Drunk as a skunk, aren't you? Tied on one too many? Can't hold your liquor, you loser."

Three of the local hoods hustled over to where Jake and the drunk lay sprawled in the foyer.

"You need some help with this dirtbag, Jake?"

Jake looked up at them. They were chomping at the bit, and he had visions of them stomping the man to death.

"It's no problem, boys. The guy is just leaving."

He bent down and whispered in the man's ear, "If you give me any grief, these *gentlemen* are liable to kill you." Jake disentangled himself from the man, who stood up on wobbly legs and left without further incident.

The hoods looked crestfallen and ambled back to their barstools. Jake bought them a round to soothe the savage beasts.

He lit a cigarette, straightened his tie, and told George to pour him a double.

HIS RELATIONSHIP WITH BRIDGET TURNED OUT not to be a one-night stand. They hooked up two or three times a week for about a month.

Then he lost interest, and he sensed she might have too.

On their last night together, he told Bridget with a straight face, "This isn't working out. I'm sorry. It's not you, it's me." Afterward he could hardly believe he'd said that, but at least he'd ended it in person, instead of over the phone or just letting it dwindle down to nothingness. She was young, Jake consoled himself, about twenty-three, and probably not what Kelly had in mind when she said it was time to get on with my life, he snorted.

SINCE HE WASN'T SEEING BRIDGET ANYMORE, he went back to keeping an eye out for hot chicks—guilt-free, now. He considered this one of his duties as manager, and it was as important to him as any other duty he had. So far, there weren't any prospects. But what the hell, he thought, it's only been two days since I said *hasta la vista* to Bridget.

THE JUDGE STOPPED IN PERIODICALLY AFTER work, and one humid summer evening, they sat down in the back of the bar to shoot the breeze.

"Pat thinks you're doing a great job," the Judge told him, "and you've got George in your corner, too."

He knew he was doing a good job, but it was still nice to know Pat and George were very satisfied with him. Thank God, George had never brought up that one incident again, and he must not have told Pat about it. While he hadn't had a drink the rest of the night after George told him off in the office, Jake had gone right back to enjoying a few gin and tonics to wet his whistle the next night. Water under the bridge, Jake thought.

As usual when he sat down to chat with the Judge or other regulars, Jake sat with his back to the wall so he could keep an eye on the place. After he and the Judge discussed the latest stunt in Washington, D.C., and solved all the world's problems, he noticed that they were getting busy. "Well, it looks like I have to go and deal with the huddled masses."

Jake pushed back his chair and started to stand up, but the Judge grabbed his arm. "Hey, are you still seeing Kelly?"

What the hell kind of question was that? "Of course. I see her every other week when I pick up the kids," he shrugged, wrenching his arm free from the Judge's surprisingly strong grip.

"You know what I'm talking about, Jake." The Judge leaned forward to deliver his message, and his expression was intense. "It's really a bad idea, and you need to move on."

Jake's initial reaction was to punch Neal's sanctimonious face, but he restrained himself. Leaning down so he was right in the Judge's face, he said, "Mind your own fucking business! Or, I'll—"

The Judge cringed. Jake didn't finish his sentence, although it was all he could do to rein himself in. He took a deep breath and let it out as the Judge hastily stood up, then hustled toward the door. As he passed by the bar, the Judge said to George, "Wow, has he changed," and thumbed his finger in Jake's direction.

George nodded but didn't say a word. The toothpick clenched between his teeth didn't move either.

Jake was only a few steps behind the Judge, but he stopped when he drew level with George. "What the fuck are you looking at?"

A shit-eating grin on his face, George gave him the finger. He still didn't say a word, but the toothpick dipped.

"Fuck you and the horse you rode in on," Jake said, grabbing the drink George had ready for him. "I just hope some asshole starts something tonight, because I have this urge to beat on someone."

As the evening wore on, he didn't get his wish. Instead, he downed a few more gin and tonics, so that by closing time, his frustration had temporarily abated. On the way home, he thought about his conversation with the Judge. "Why did I go off on him like I did?"

He answered himself, "Because I can't let go of Kelly." He shook his head and swore again.

He knew he probably should call the Judge tomorrow and apologize for his outburst. After all, if weren't for the Judge, he wouldn't have this job. And they'd been friends since third grade.

The lines on the road kept moving and weaving from side to side, and Jake realized he had to concentrate on his driving. The last thing he needed was to be pulled over by the cops for drunk driving. He'd almost made it home when he heard the siren.

Oh, fuck, he thought, pulling over. He was going to get arrested.

The cop asked him for his license and registration. Jake groped around in the glove box for the registration, then hauled out his wallet to give the officer his license.

The officer took both items, looked at them, then said, "Step out of the car, Mr. Sherman."

He was fucked. He was really fucked.

The officer asked Jake to walk a straight line. He did it, somehow. Then the officer asked him to recite the alphabet backwards. Miracle of miracles, Jake did it by visualizing the alphabet and saying it backwards slowly.

The cop was impressed. "Even though you passed the tests, I know you're drunk, and you stink. However, I see by your driver's license that you only live a block from here. I'm going to drive you home. You can pick up your car tomorrow."

Jake sighed in relief and hoped the cop didn't change his mind before Jake get home.

Jake got in the front passenger seat of the car. The officer said, "You'd better not puke in here!"

"No, sirrr," Jake said, trying not to slur his words. The officer rolled his eyes and drove him home.

Jake got out of the car and tried to lean down to look in the window at the cop. He was a bit unsteady on his feet, but he managed to say, "Pleeash wait, off'cer. I wan' to give you somethin'."

He staggered into the house and came out with some free drink tickets for the Poodle. He stumbled and fell on the hood of the patrol car, and struggled to stand upright again.

The cop, disgusted, put his car in reverse and drove away.

Jake yelled after him, "Wait, I have free ticketsh!" His arm outstretched, the tickets clutched in his fist, Jake watched the patrol car drive away, surprised the cop didn't want them.

Once the taillights disappeared around the corner. He spread out his arms and shouted to no one in particular, "Well, that'sh gra-gratitude for ya!"

ONE AFTERNOON WHEN JAKE ARRIVED AT work, four off-duty cops—including MacPherson—were drinking at the bar. Jake moved in closer so he could hear their conversation. He enjoyed being around the cops and often thought what it would've been like if he had become one. Interesting, no doubt, especially the detective work, although his fascination was probably the result of watching one too many Clint Eastwood movies, he conceded.

The other three cops were regulars at the Poodle, so he felt comfortable joining them. When he got close enough, he heard one of them say the word 'murder'.

"The victim was only eighteen, poor kid," Jim Ferguson said.

Jake gave MacPherson a friendly punch hello, and nodded at Ferguson and the other two. "Did I hear you guys talking about a murder?

"Yup," one of them said glumly.

Jake asked, "Do you have any suspects yet?"

"Oh, they know who did it," Frank said, slamming his fist on the bar. "That piece of shit, Lucky Doyle. Problem is, he has two of his hookers giving him an alibi."

I knew that bastard was no good, Jake thought. One of the other cops gave Jake a run down of Doyle's criminal record, some of which Jake already knew. "During his long life full of crime, he's had seven arrests—pimping, selling drugs, assault, robbery, and a murder charge that was knocked down to manslaughter. All in all, he's been in the joint about eleven years, give or take."

Jake broke out in a sweat, thinking about his Doyle nightmare. *Fuck.* "How'd the bastard kill her?"

Ferguson replied, "With a knife of some sort. She was sliced up pretty good. And the prick is probably going to walk." He shook his head and finished his drink in one long swig.

The conversation shifted to talking about pussy and other important matters of the day, but Jake didn't join in. He couldn't get his head around what he had just heard. How could the cops be so nonchalant about the killing?

Jake nudged Frank and they walked away from the group.

"What the fuck? That's it? You guys are giving up, and Doyle's gonna walk?" he glared at Frank.

Frank put his hand on Jake's shoulder. "Listen, Jake, calm down. This isn't like the movies. Lots of murders don't get solved in real life. And, yes, even when you know who did it."

"I can't accept that this slimeball is going to get away with it. Someone ought to put a bullet in him."

Frank raised his eyebrows. "I don't know why you're so upset about this. Care to enlighten me?"

Jake shook his fist. "Frank, I just know that guy is the devil. He's evil, and now this murder confirms that. Besides, I've seen him talking to Dawn, and I'm worried about her."

"Dawn who? Who are you talking about?"

Jake told him more about the Doyle and Dawn situation.

Frank grimaced. "Not much can be done about it. Just keep an eye on her."

"I will. So, Frank, promise me, you'll keep me updated on the investigation."

Frank shrugged and replied, "I'm not officially part of this one, but I'll do what I can."

Jake walked to the other end of the bar and related what the police had said to George.

George replied, "It's not our concern, Dick Tracy. We've got enough to worry about."

AFTER A NIGHT OFF, JAKE ALWAYS CHECKED with George to see if anything unusual had occurred in his absence.

Before he even got to George that night, the waitress—nicknamed Mansfield —approached Jake and said, "I thought you'd want to know that Dawn left here with Lucky last night."

"What the fuck! I'm gone one weekend, and this happens." His hands balled into fists, and he felt his face flush. He'd tried to catch up with Dawn the night he heard about the murder so he could warn her again, but she'd avoided him and scooted out as soon as her shift ended at 10 p.m.

Not bothering to thank Mansfield for the info, he turned on his heel and hurried over to George. "How could you let this happen?" he demanded.

"What the fuck are you talking about?" George frowned.

Jake relayed what Mansfield had said.

George snorted, "I'm not a babysitter." He continued mixing a martini. "You're the one who hired her. If anything bad happens to her, let it be on your head."

Jake stormed away, disgusted. George could be such an asshole. He'd have to handle this himself, and talk some hard sense into Dawn. He glanced around the Poodle and spotted her across the room, taking an order. He strode up to her and grabbed her arm. "Let's go to the office. I want to talk to you! Now!"

Her eyes widened, and she let him lead her toward the office. "You're hurting me, Mr. Sherman."

What he really should do is put her over his knee and spank some sense into her. Instead he let go of her arm.

Jake closed the door behind them. He was not happy about having to do this again, so he really got in her face this time, planting himself only inches away from her.

"I promised your dad I'd watch out for you," he growled, "and it appears you haven't listened to anything I've said about that bum, Doyle. I've told you that he is a pimp and a drug dealer, and now he's a definite suspect in the murder of a girl your age."

Her mouth opened in shock. Tears ran down Dawn's face. She was crying, but he wasn't sure why. Then her eyes narrowed, she sniffed angrily, and her innocent expression turned defensive. "I'm over eighteen. I can make my own decisions," she shot back at him, threw open the door, and all but ran out of the office. Jake was taken aback by her reaction. Doyle really had her under his spell. Things had gone farther than he'd thought. He decided, then and there, he would have to do something about Doyle.

As he left the office and walked back into the bar, he saw Hector Lopez bellied up to the bar.

"And there's another problem I'll have to take care of eventually," he muttered, frustrated. Hopefully not tonight, but he was in no mood to put up with this guy's mouth.

Hector Lopez was in his late twenties. The guy was a wiry little piece of shit who used to fight in the Golden Gloves. Jake outweighed him by at least twenty pounds and was four inches taller. Lopez didn't come in too often, but when he did, Jake found him really annoying. Hector delighted in taking verbal shots at Jake for whatever reason, and he liked to challenge Jake on all manner of things.

That evening, Lopez mouthed off more than usual and made the mistake of punching Jake in the shoulder—probably as a way to antagonize Jake and get a reaction out of him.

Jake had always tried to ignore him in the past, but now, something in him snapped. He exploded. His fists came up and he went toe to toe with Hector.

As George told him later, the fight actually did look like two guys in a ring, duking it out. "You both looked pretty good. I decided not to break it up as long as you weren't getting the worst of it."

The fight eventually subsided when Jake knocked Lopez down. Lopez came up quickly and then when Jake knocked him down again, he held up his hands and indicated he quit.

It took some time for Jake's heart rate to get back to normal. He went to the bathroom and surveyed his face and hands. Fortunately, he hadn't broken anything this time. He looked in the mirror at his unscathed face and said, "Don't mess with The Jake!" He was pretty sure Hector Lopez would never come back to the Poodle—it'd be too embarrassing for him.

Jake was proud of how well he'd done—the only blood on his clothes was Hector's. His confidence rose several notches. He felt he could win any fight. And he knew who he wanted to fight more than anyone. "You're next, Doyle."

CHAPTER 15

Wednesday, August 1

JAKE NOTICED LUCKY DOYLE ENTER THE Poodle and take a seat at a booth—unusual for Doyle, who usually hung out at the bar. Jake thought for a moment and wasn't at all surprised when he realized Doyle had chosen a table in Dawn's section. This was the first time he'd seen Doyle in the bar since warning Dawn about his criminal background.

After serving Doyle a drink, Dawn remained by the table, chatting with Doyle and the disheveled guy he'd brought into the Poodle with him. Obviously, she chose to ignore Jake's warning.

Before he could stop himself, Jake strode over to the booth. "Dawn, go take care of the rest of your customers. They look thirsty," he said to her while glaring at Doyle.

Dawn scurried away. Jake leaned on the table and bent forward so his face was nearly level with Doyle's. "Stay the fuck away from her, or—"

"Or what, Jew boy?" Lucky said, leaning back in the booth, looking relaxed and in control of the situation.

"I know what you are, asshole, and I know what you did," Jake shot back, then straightened.

Doyle leaned forward. "Get outta my face. The only thing keeping me from beating the shit out of you is him." Doyle jerked his thumb at George, who was approaching the booth, an intent look on his face and the toothpick clenched a little more tightly than usual between his teeth.

George caught the eye of the other man with Doyle. "Take him the fuck out of here, now," he said, indicating Doyle.

Doyle looked at his silent, burly companion, rolled his eyes, and nodded once.

They stood up and headed toward the door. Before Doyle had gone more than a few feet, he stopped and looked over his shoulder at Jake. "Don't let me catch you without your babysitter," he sneered.

"Don't let that stop you," Jake replied, clenching his fists as George pushed his rigid body farther away from Doyle.

Doyle laughed and left with the other guy. Jake's hands were still clenched, his nails digging into his palms.

George took one look at him and told him to go sit at the bar. Without saying a word, Jake followed George's instructions and mindlessly gulped down the gin and tonic George set before him. He knew if he said anything, he'd explode. The fury would spill out and he wouldn't be able to stuff it back inside.

George poured him a second one. "You got balls, Jake, but no brains. I know you took Hector Lopez apart, but this is a whole different cat."

A HALF HOUR LATER, JAKE SAID TO George, "I'm just going to go outside and get some fresh air."

Jake was still seeing red; he couldn't forget about the confrontation with Doyle, and he hoped Doyle would pass by or even return to the Poodle. He patted his lower back to make sure his ebony club was tucked into his belt and easily accessible. He envisioned smashing Doyle's face with the club while Doyle was on the ground, having been leveled by a couple of blows from Jake. He had his gun, too, of course, but beating the shit out of Doyle with his fists and the club sounded a lot more satisfying.

Jake stepped out the front door. The sun was setting, but it was still hot and muggy. He lit a cigarette and looked up toward the heavens. The moon would be full in a few days and that meant the crazies would be out in full force again.

He gradually calmed down as he puffed on his Winston, enjoying his escape from the insanity of the Poodle for a few minutes.

He looked at his watch. Eight thirty. His shift was only half over. How could he keep doing this, night after night? Was there an end in sight? What would happen between him and Doyle?

He smiled wryly and said to no one in particular, "God has seen fit to punish me for my sins, now, instead of waiting for my death. He has sentenced me to hell, disguised as the Poodle."

A disheveled man approached and caught his eye. Jake sniffed and drew back. The bum smelled like he had been sleeping with dead fish.

"Excuse me, sir, could you spare me some change?"

Six months ago, Jake would have given the guy a couple of bucks and encouraged him not to use the money for booze. But after working at the den of iniquity, Jake had nothing but disdain for this creature. He had developed a cynical attitude toward drunks. The liberalism he'd espoused when he started this job had all but disappeared.

"Hey, this side of the street belongs to me!" Jake growled. "You can work the other side."

The man scurried away. Jake ground out his cigarette and went back inside.

HE SURVEYED THE ROOM, NOTICING THE dregs of humanity lurking on barstools, in booths, and at tables. God, he was sick of this hellhole.

He sat down at the bar, planning to do some serious drinking.

Aww, hell. Who was he kidding? I'm just like them, he thought as he signaled to George.

With his back to the room for perhaps the first time since he started at the Poodle, Jake ignored the crowd and focused on the double gin and tonic George put in front of him.

He lit up another cigarette, wishing he could be anywhere but here. He'd especially like to be with Kelly, but the more he sung this song, the more he realized the futility of their relationship. It'd been weeks since he'd spent the night.

His mind wandered to his kids. He still had more than a week before his weekend off of work, but even then, he wouldn't get to see them, Kelly had said, because she was taking them out of town to another event with her side of the family. He gripped the glass tighter as he hoped that's what was really happening, and not that she was dating some guy who was planning on being at the house all weekend. Or, worse, taking them away for the weekend.

Jake sighed, knowing it was pointless to think about Kelly with another man. He signaled George for a refill.

He'd lost contact with all his old friends, and he missed them. None of them ever came to the Poodle. He'd pretty much given up trying to reach them by phone; it was too hard to keep in contact with them because of his crazy work hours.

His pack of cigarettes was empty, and he told anyone who would listen, "Hey, I need another pack of cigarettes over here." A minute later, someone put a fresh pack in front of him. Was . . . was that two packs of cigarettes, or was he seeing double? The room was starting to spin. He really had to concentrate on not falling off his stool as he tilted his head back and emptied the glass.

He took stock of everything that was going to hell in his life and catalogued all his woes. But after a while, he lost track of them, so he just quit thinking.

He raised his arm and motioned George over. "Gimme 'nother one."

George raised his eyebrow at Jake. "You sure you can handle another one?"

"Yeah. Make it a d-double this time . . . this time. And keep 'em comin.'"

George just shrugged, mixed the drink, and slid it across the bar to Jake.

Jake lit another cigarette but had trouble finding his mouth with it. *Goddammit.* He kept trying.

A little while later, George announced, "We've closed fifteen minutes ago, Jake, and I did your work for you. Now I'm going to put you to bed at the Anthony so you can sleep this off. You're in no condition to drive home."

Jake was vaguely aware that George half dragged him up some stairs.

"It's 'nother fine mess I'm in, Ollie," he mumbled to George as he landed facedown on a bed that wouldn't stop moving.

The next morning brought the mother of all hangovers, and more embarrassment than he could stomach. After puking half the morning in the hotel room's toilet, he snuck out of the Hotel Anthony and headed home to get cleaned up . . . then head back to work to start the daily grind again.

Fuck. I can't do this much longer.

SOON AFTER JAKE ARRIVED AT WORK on Friday, Pat mentioned to him, "Dawn's father called me last night. He said she hadn't come home, and he was worried. You and I know she was probably just out partying, but when she finally gets her ass in here today for her shift, tell her to call home."

Jake swallowed hard. His mouth grew dry. He strode into the office, looked up Dawn's home phone number in the personnel file, and dialed.

A sense of foreboding filled him as he listened to the phone ring.

"Hello?" the father answered.

"Mr. Pilger, this is Jake Sherman at the Poodle. Has Dawn shown up yet? Because she hasn't come to work today. She's almost a half-hour late."

"No, she hasn't come home," the father said tightly.

"Have you called the police?"

"Yes, but they told me that until she's been missing for twenty-four hours—they have to wait that long because she's considered an adult now that she's eighteen—I can't file a missing person's report," he said, frustration and weariness evident in his voice. "I don't know what to do; I've called all her friends . . . her mother's in church, praying, and I don't know what to do. This isn't like Dawn at all."

A sour taste filled his mouth as an image of Dawn with Doyle flashed through his mind, but he tried not to go there. Thinking the worst wouldn't help the situation.

He took a deep breath. "If you hear anything, let me know. And I'll do likewise." He hung up.

A cold chill made him shiver, and he went directly to the bar, where he lit up a Winston with hands that shook only a little. "George, bring me a gin and tonic."

Chewing on his trusty toothpick, George brought it and asked, "What's up?"

Jake told him but left out his worry about Doyle. "And I don't know what to do. Shall I call Frank to see if he can find out anything?"

"I think you're overreacting," George said, moving the tooth-pick from one side of his mouth to the other.

"What do you mean, I'm overreacting? This is definitely not like her. She's a good kid," Jake said, agitated that George didn't understand the situation. Why the fuck was he the only one who was concerned?

George brushed him off. "I got work to do, and so do you." He turned his back and walked down the length of the bar to serve a customer at the far end.

Jake knocked back the drink. George was partially right. There was nothing he could do right now. He decided not to call Frank—it was too hard to reach him—and Frank was due in that night, anyway, for his shift as a bouncer.

He hoped he wasn't overreacting . . . but his instincts told him something terrible had happened.

A LITTLE LATER IN THE EVENING, Jake told a drunk customer that he'd had enough to drink and then asked him to leave. The guy actually agreed and left without any problem.

Will wonders never cease, Jake thought.

He walked over to the bar and said to George, "Maybe we'll have a quiet evening and not have to bust some heads."

"Every time you say that, we have something big go down." George sounded resigned.

Jake laughed, turned, and saw . . . a vision. A beautiful woman had walked into the bar. She is drop-dead gorgeous, he thought.

About five foot six, jet-black hair, and legs that wouldn't quit. She was dressed like she was going to a gala. For sure, she seemed out of place here.

She caught Jake's eye and walked directly up to him. "Are you the manager?"

He was perplexed. What was broad like her doing in a place like the Poodle and asking for the manager, no less?

"Yes. How can I help you?" He gave her his most charming smile.

She looked him in the eye. "I've never fucked a bar manager. You could be the first."

Jake did a double take but tried not to show it. He'd seen and heard things here at the Poodle that defied the imagination, but this took the cake—and it sounded to him like she wanted him for dessert. He hung onto his composure but couldn't think of a clever response. He was normally quick on his feet, but this one really took him off his game.

Much to his surprise, he replied, "I appreciate the offer, but I think I'll pass."

She shrugged, walked over to the bar, and sat down on a barstool, her back to him.

He watched her, and said to himself, What did I just do? Am I fucking nuts? I just turned down a great piece of ass!

Mansfield tugged on his sleeve. "Hey, I'm busting my butt here tonight, covering for Dawn. You gonna pay me double time?" She grinned.

"Go fuck yourself," he laughed.

"Back at ya, *Mister* Sherman," she retorted as she reached to gather dirty glasses from an empty table.

He went back to studying the beautiful woman and tried to figure out why he'd turned her down. She wasn't interested in him; he was just another notch on her belt. It dawned on him that this was what a woman must feel like when a jerk like him tried to hit on her.

This time it was Nick, the extra bartender, who grabbed his attention, calling him over. Leaning across the bar, Nick whispered, "See that fox sitting in my station? She just asked me to fuck her tonight!"

He nodded slowly. "Let me guess, she told you she'd never fucked a bartender before."

Nick was flabbergasted. "How did you know?"

Jake smiled. "The Jake knows everything."

Driving home that night, he realized he didn't know if Nick had left with the woman or not, and he really didn't care. He wondered how many guys tried to hit on Kelly. It incensed him to think about it. Jake promised himself that he'd respect women more. Then he grinned, relishing the idea of telling Kelly this story. She'd get a kick out of it. And maybe she'd be impressed with him saying no to the woman.

It also occurred to him that he had turned down Miss Hot Legs because he just wasn't in the mood. The whole Dawn thing was really eating at him.

He sighed and pulled into his driveway.

WHEN JAKE HAD SEEN FRANK ON SATURDAY NIGHT, the cop hadn't had anything to report about Dawn's disappearance. Jake felt sick to his stomach, but he tried to keep up a good front for the customers. Besides, George and Frank thought he was overreacting anyway.

So when he saw Frank entering the bar on Monday evening, he was somewhat surprised, since Frank was not on duty as the bouncer. Jake called him over for a drink and tried to act casual, despite his worry about Dawn. "So what's up, my man? How are they hanging?"

Frank didn't smile.

Jake asked, "What's wrong?"

"I have some very bad news for you."

Jake tensed. "Does this have anything to do with Dawn?"

"I'm afraid so. Brace yourself, man. They found her. She was murdered and the detectives told me it was not a pretty sight."

The muscles in Jake's face twitched and tightened. Bile rose in his throat and he nearly gagged. He pounded on the bar with his fists and yelled a guttural cry, which sounded loud even to his own ears. The bar suddenly grew very still as everyone looked at him.

"Calm down, Jake," George advised, suddenly appearing in Jake's narrow vision. "The veins in your neck are throbbing; you're going to have a fucking stroke if you don't settle down." George poured him a gin with a little tonic splashed on top, and said, "Drink this. For crissakes, Jake, calm down."

George's words barely penetrated the grief and anger whirling inside him. He snarled, "I don't want to fucking calm down. I want to hit somebody. No, I want to kill somebody!"

"If you can handle it, I'll give you some of the details," Frank said, grabbing Jake's shoulder. "She—"

Jake interrupted him. "I know who did it. Lucky Doyle! Go arrest the bastard!"

Frank leveled a condescending gaze at him. "The department is looking at Doyle as a person of interest. But, as I've told you before, this isn't the movies or TV, Jake. You have to have evidence before you arrest someone."

Jake let out a frustrated breath. "I don't give a shit about evidence. I know that sick sonofabitch killed her. What are you guys gonna do?" Anger coursed through him as he ground out the words. Nausea threatened to overwhelm him again.

Frank sat back. "First of all, I don't have anything to do with the investigation, but I know the detectives who have been assigned to the case, and I promise you I'll keep you informed."

Jake shook his head and walked away, leaving his drink untouched. He could barely function that night. He felt a debilitating sense of guilt toward her father and especially toward her. If he hadn't hired her, she wouldn't be dead. His jaw was clenched and his movements jerky as he went through the motions of working.

Later, George called him over, poured him a drink, and said sympathetically, "Maybe this will help change your mood."

Jake ignored the drink as his gut wrenched. He put his hand on his revolver, and said, "George, I'm telling ya. If the police don't get Doyle, I will."

CHAPTER 16

Thursday, August 9

J AKE KNEW HE WAS OBSESSING, but he couldn't get out of his
mind the image described by the cops of the crime scene and
of the condition of Dawn's body. And of Doyle, with that perma-
nent smirk on his craggy face. He remembered the warnings he'd
given Dawn to stay away from Doyle; in hindsight, he regretted
not firing her, maybe then she would still be alive. He was full of
self-recriminations. With a constant, splitting headache, he just
couldn't think about anything else.

He spent the next few days anxiously awaiting any news regarding the case.

Nothing.

ON THE FOLLOWING FRIDAY, FRANK SHOWED up for his shift as
bouncer at five p.m. sharp. Jake cornered him when he walked in
the door. "Any news?"

"You're not going to like this, but, so far they haven't turned up
anything. No witnesses, and nothing to incriminate Doyle or con-
nect him to the crime."

"So that's it?" Jake said, disgusted with this turn of events. He'd
pictured Doyle already in custody. "They're not going to do anything
about this? I know that sonofabitch killed her, dammit! What the
hell's the matter with you people?" He slammed his hand on the bar.

"Hey, with all due respect," Frank responded, "you just don't seem to understand how the system works. Get a grip, man. They're doing everything they can, but the fact is that if you don't turn up leads within the first week or two, chances are slim you ever will."

"So, what are you telling me? They're pulling people off the case?" He was shocked.

"I don't know all the details. I just told you what I knew," Frank answered, heading back to the office to punch in on the time clock.

"Shit," Jake said out loud. "Shit. Goddammit." He felt his face flush with anger, and he looked around for someone to punch. He swallowed his frustration instead and waved George over, "Another one."

George poured him the drink.

Jake opened his mouth to let loose his frustration about the cops, but before he got a word out, George held up his hand. "I don't want to discuss this with you right now. I'm busy." George headed to the other end of the bar, obviously sick of hearing Jake talk about it.

Jake looked around the Poodle. Was he fucking crazy? Was he the only one who gave a shit? He kicked the bottom of the bar, stubbing his toe. Fuck all of them. If they wouldn't do something about this, he would. He would investigate Doyle on his own.

JAKE CAUGHT HIS MIND WANDERING AS he sat in the office, trying to make up the next day's liquor order for Pat. He couldn't keep his mind off the idea of going after Doyle himself, and he pondered how he would go about it. He realized that he didn't know squat, even though he had watched at least a hundred detective movies and read as many books. When Jake had attempted to learn some things from Frank, the response had been patronizing. "Jake, you should leave this to the professionals."

George, on the other hand, had taken him seriously. "Jake, if Doyle finds out you've been snooping around, he just might kill *you*."

He would go forward anyway, because nailing Doyle for Dawn's murder had become a full-blown mission. It occupied all his thoughts, night and day, and made it difficult to concentrate on anything else.

He decided to start by cruising the bars to find some of the girls that worked for Doyle. He would get them to talk. What he needed was a witness—that was his goal. He would do it early afternoons, before he began his shift and when the girls were most likely to be available.

And so what if Lucky found out. The idea made him smile.

Yes! If Doyle came for him, he'd have a reason to kill the bastard. With that happy thought, he left the office and said to George, "Hit me, my friend, and make it a double."

JAKE HAD SATURDAY NIGHT OFF AND agreed to stay at the house to babysit the children while Kelly went on a date. He didn't mind too much, as it gave him more time with Sarah and Sean. Also a plus— he could see what Kelly's date looked like. And, he said to himself mischievously, *I* plan on being the one who spends the night—not this other guy.

Jake arrived and, after a brief conversation with Kelly, she went upstairs to get ready. The children were busy watching TV and Jake started dinner before going downstairs to bring up the laundry.

As he took the clothes out of the dryer, he picked up a robe of Kelly's and had a brilliant idea. If he could, he'd stop this date before it even began. He grinned. *It's not me—it's the devil making me do this.*

He stripped, put on Kelly's robe, and climbed the stairs just as the doorbell rang. His timing was perfect. He answered the door and held it wide open. "Would you like to come in?"

The expression on the guy's face was somewhere between shocked and disbelief as he eyed Jake up and down. Trying not to bust out laughing, Jake said, "Don't just stand there. Are you coming in, or not?"

The man turned on his heel and left, muttering obscenities to himself.

Jake ran downstairs, put his clothes back on, and eagerly trotted up the stairs to the kitchen to wait for Kelly. She might need consoling because her date had changed his mind.

JAKE ARRIVED AT WORK ON MONDAY in a decent mood. He'd spent the afternoon combing bars, looking for Doyle's girls and found a few. While none of them had anything worthwhile to say, he was still hopeful he'd find someone who would.

As usual, his thoughts turned to Kelly and he fantasized about them getting back together. He'd have to be proactive about it, however, because he knew she was having some other new guy over for dinner tonight.

He tried to think of ways that he could fuck up this evening, too, for her, as he had on Saturday, and he came up with another brilliant idea.

He figured out when they would be eating and, knowing that if the phone rang, it would probably be Sean picking up, Jake called.

Sure enough, Sean answered the phone.

"Sean, listen to me. This is your father. I want you to yell out to mom that Jake wants to know if she found the pair of tennis shoes he had left here last night."

Jake chuckled as he listened to Sean follow his instructions perfectly.

Kelly came to the phone and said with a smile in her voice, "You sonofabitch, you've done it again!"

"I love you too," Jake said, grinning, and hung up. It was the only bright spot in an otherwise frustrating day.

CHAPTER 17

Monday, September 10

ABOUT SEVEN P.M., JAKE NOTICED TWO GIRLS AT THE BAR. They looked about sixteen or seventeen and were sitting on either side of a paunchy guy in his forties who Jake had never seen before. The girls were dressed up, and the guy had on a white shirt, dark pants, and a tweedy sport coat. He looked like he'd just gotten off work. George was busy getting drinks at the other end of the bar, so Jake walked over and asked the girls for ID.

Before the girls could respond, the man pulled out his wallet and flashed a detective's badge. "They're with me, so don't worry about it," he said dismissively, turning away from Jake and toward the nervous-looking girl on his right.

What was up with this putz? Jake smiled and stuck out his hand. "I'm Jake Sherman, the manager, and I didn't get your name."

The detective swung around to face Jake and barked, "Jerry Kroll. Now go fucking bother somebody else."

Cops weren't high on Jake's list right now, especially one with two underage girls in tow. He wasn't about to take any shit from this guy. "If they don't have any ID, we won't serve them or you," he said in a deceptively calm voice.

Detective Kroll surged off his barstool, planted himself in Jake's face, and stopped just short of poking a finger at Jake's chest. "For the last time, they're with me and that should be good enough," he yelled.

Jake's temper flared and his heart rate quickened. He held his stance and didn't back down or move away. He glared at Kroll. "How do I know that you're not trying to set us up for serving a minor?" Jake thought that it wasn't likely, but it made a nice retort. George had come down to their end of the bar and, with that stupid toothpick hanging out of his mouth, he grinned like Goofy. George was with him on this.

Jake stared into the cop's pale eyes. "You know, on second thought, why don't you just take these broads and get the fuck out of my bar?" he challenged.

Kroll looks furious enough to hit me, he thought, and clenched his fists. Just give me an excuse, you asshole, he added silently. With his right hand, he reached around under his sport coat for his club, but the detective stepped back. Kroll looked around the room and clearly noticed he was the center of attention.

He grabbed the girls' arms and hustled them toward the door. As he exited, he turned and looked at Jake, "Someday, I will have the opportunity to make you regret this evening."

After Kroll and the girls left the bar, George said to Jake, "Your balls are bigger than your brain! You are one crazy mother fucker. You just pissed off a big shot in the police department."

"Fuck him. I'm running this place and he can take a flying fuck, for all I care!" Jake tapped the counter. "Pour me a drink. George." He downed it and said, "Hit me again."

By the time he finished his second drink, he calmed down. He thought about what had just happened and wondered if he had gone too far. He'd been told that if a cop wanted to get you, he could always find a way.

Later that evening a small group of men drifted in that Jake pegged as off-duty cops. They introduced themselves as colleagues of Frank MacPherson's. Jake welcomed them, and bought them all a drink, as he often did when the cops came in. To Jake's surprise, they had already heard of the incident with Kroll.

A tall, wiry Swedish-looking cop spoke up. "We heard you stuck it to that prick, Kroll. Couldn't happen to a nicer guy," he guffawed. He slapped Jake on the back.

Another cop chimed in. "Everybody hates that asshole, and you don't have to worry about him getting back at you. You've got a lot of friends on the force, and after tonight, you have many more. We just wish we could've been here to watch the fucker squirm."

The officers laughed and toasted Jake with their bottles of Hamm's.

His conversation with the cops put Jake's mind at ease. He'd done the right thing. He just hoped Kroll didn't take out his frustration on the girls. He wondered why they were with him in the first place; they looked like good kids.

When he could work it into conversation, he asked the cops if they had any news about Dawn's murder.

"No. You're probably better off asking Frank about that," the Swede said.

Despite not getting any information about Dawn's case, Jake still counted the night as a win. He had done the right thing with Kroll and made a few new friends on the police force. You never know when that can come in handy, he thought.

ON ONE BALMY NIGHT IN MID-SEPTEMBER, Carl stuck around past his usual 10 p.m. The Old Man didn't normally hang out 'til closing, but occasionally he would. Jake hated it; it felt like the Old Man was checking up on him. Besides, it cramped Jake's ability to pick up women.

Damn. Carl was going to spoil Jake's action with Gretchen if he stayed there until they closed.

But Jake wasn't about to be deterred. He'd met Gretchen for the first time tonight; she'd come in late and he had to put the moves on her fast. So far, so good. She was at the bar, nursing a drink, and he leaned on the counter next to her. She laughed in all the right places in his stories, and smiled at him a lot. He'd staked his claim and so everyone left her alone.

Now, to close the deal, he needed her to stick around after closing. Once they had some more booze, and assuming she said yes, he'd take her to a room in the Anthony. Everything about her said she was interested.

Lighting another smoke, he revised his plan and spoke to her in a low voice. "At ten minutes to one, I want you to go downstairs to the ladies room, go into one of the stalls, latch the door closed, and stand on the toilet seat."

"Are you serious?" She looked taken aback.

"Think of it as an adventure," Jake grinned. "When you hear the Old Man"—Jake discreetly pointed out white-haired Carl—"enter the room to check it, you need to crouch down until he leaves."

She started to protest, but as he walked away, he turned, winked at her, and said, "Do it." She shrugged and grinned.

Ahh. This was going to work. Jake was delighted with another of his cockamamy plans.

Closing went smoothly for a change and, looking around, he didn't see Gretchen anywhere. He thought that either she had left or, he smiled, she was standing on the stinking toilet seat.

As predicted, Carl went downstairs. Jake listened to him check the men's room, then the women's. All was quiet, and Carl said nothing when he came upstairs. A minute later, he said good night and left. George and Leonard had already left, too, so Jake had the place to himself.

Jake gave out a little whoopee, locked the doors, and went downstairs to see if Gretchen had stayed. He tried to get into the ladies room, but the goddamned door was locked. This had never happened before.

Gretchen called, "Is that you, Jake?"

"Yeah, it's me," he replied. "But the door seems to be locked. Can you unlock it from your side?"

After pushing and pulling and turning the knob for several minutes, they had no success. She started to panic; her voice got all high-pitched and it sounded like a bout of hysteria was in the works.

"Calm down, Gretchen," he said in his most soothing voice. "I'm going upstairs to try and locate the key. I'll be right back."

He rummaged through the desk drawers, looked in the safe for an extra set of keys, and dug through the papers on the desk. No key. Where was the damn thing? The only possibility was that Carl had accidentally put it in his pocket. Or, maybe he did it on purpose.

Okay, God, it is apparent to me that you don't intend for me to get laid tonight.

Jake sighed and went back downstairs to talk to Gretchen through the door. He hoped she was calmer.

Eventually, Jake got her out after picking the lock. It took him half an hour, but he did it. When she finally got out, she threw herself into his arms. He took her back upstairs into the Poodle and poured drinks for both of them, then lit a cigarette for himself. She did the same. A few swallows of alcohol and she seemed back to normal. By their second round, they were both laughing about it.

Now, he wondered, should he take her over to the Anthony to get laid? He didn't feel like walking that far. He looked around the empty Poodle and decided, "Aw, hell. This place is as good as any."

JAKE'S INVESTIGATION TOOK HIM TO SEVERAL BARS on Hennepin Avenue for two or three hours every day. He ordered a drink at each bar, but he didn't always finish them because he was trying to keep his wits about him.

So far, he had come up with nothing. Girls weren't talking; it seemed they were scared to death of Lucky.

He decided to talk to Jose. The half-black, half-Mexican was as rough and tough-looking as any heavy he'd ever seen in a movie, which had sure worked to Jake's advantage with the four black kids a few months back.

He found Jose at the Gay Ninety's, a strip joint on Sixth and Hennepin. He approached him, and after a little bullshit conversation, Jake asked, "What's your take on Lucky Doyle?"

Jose's eyes narrowed. If anything, his gravelly voice got even deeper. "Don't like the Mutter fucker, he white trash. Why do you ask?"

"I think he killed one of my waitresses."

"I'd take him out for you, but I'm too damn old to spend any more time in the slammer. But iffin he come after *you*, I'll take him out." Jose nodded, as if to emphasize his offer.

Jake told Jose that so far that wasn't the case, but he appreciated the man's concern.

Jose shrugged. "Take care o' yourself, man. 'Member, ya need a favor, ya find me," he said in that guttural voice that Jake—and everyone else—could barely understand. "S'pose I could give ya some names of hookers that might know somethin.'"

"Hell, yes," Jake said. He had a second drink while he wrote down the names Jose told him. Jake was hopeful. This could be his first break.

A little later, he left the strip joint and headed to the Poodle. He was due there soon anyway.

He was fucking glad Jose was a friend. He wouldn't want the man for an enemy. He shook his head. War made strange bedfellows.

JAKE WALKED UP AND DOWN THE BAR on what felt like an ordinary Monday evening, buying the guys drinks. He overheard a conversation between a couple of regulars—local hoods, actually—talking about Tricky Dicky.

Jake joined in. "What a bastard Nixon is."

One of the hoods said, "Well, he's not the only one. I could tell ya stories about Minnesota's favorite son, Hubert Humphrey, the former vice president."

Jake's interest was piqued. "Tell me more. Tell me, tell me," he said and handed them each another drink.

Jake noticed one hood giving the other a dirty look, as if to say, "What'd ya open up your big mouth for?"

Jake decided to push them. He was bored and in the mood for a good story about Minneapolis's famous politician. "Come on, don't stop now. I'm interested."

The taller of the two—the one with pockmarks scattered across his face—settled in on his stool and lit up a cigarette. "Okay. Do you remember a guy named Freddie Gates?"

Jake replied, "Of course. He was Humphrey's right-hand man. He died, though, didn't he?"

The guy nodded. "Yup. A couple of years ago, Freddie Gates died and all the big shots from all over the country attended his funeral here, including Hubert Humphrey and, of course, the Secret Service. Here's the deal—and you didn't hear it from me.

Gates' grandkids—they were teenagers at the time—stayed at home to watch the place while everyone else attended the funeral. Three guys, who will remain nameless, broke into the house, tied up the kids, and emptied the safe."

Not fucking likely. Jake said sarcastically, "Yeah, right. Where do you get this bullshit from?"

The shorter guy with the bad teeth said, "Well, if you don't believe us, ask your buddy . . . the Judge."

Jake had had enough. He walked away, thinking, These two guys are just full of shit. But he couldn't get rid of the nagging idea that the Judge was somehow involved in the story. Those two losers telling the tale seemed pretty sure.

A couple nights later, the Judge came in. Seeing him reminded Jake of the story the two hoods had told.

Jake said, "Hey, I want to talk to you. I heard this story about Gates and Humphrey." Jake related what he'd heard.

The Judge appeared shocked. "Who told you that?"

"What's the difference?" Jake said, shrugging a shoulder. "What do you know about it?"

The Judge tried to change the subject, but Jake continued to press him until he gave in. "Well, okay, I'll tell you, but you got to promise—*promise*—me that this will never, ever go any further, for both your sake and for mine."

"Oh, yeah, fine, I swear," Jake promised impatiently. "Just give me the story."

The Judge confirmed the story that three guys robbed the house during the funeral and emptied the contents of the safe. "They took a quarter of a million out of the safe, and some papers."

Jake interrupted, "How do you know so much about this?"

"The Humphrey people let it be known that the robbers could keep the money—they just wanted the papers back—and there would be no further investigation. And the reason I know so much about it is because I was the go-between."

This didn't really add up, Jake thought. "What was in the papers?"

"Obviously, something they didn't want made public," the

Judge said. He whispered a few details to Jake, then said in a normal voice, "Hey, get me another drink, will ya?"

The Judge was obviously trying to distract him from asking for more specifics, but Jake wouldn't let it go as he signaled Mansfield, the young waitress with the big knockers, to bring another round of drinks. "Well, so whatever happened? Did they get the papers back?"

"Yeah, they did. They recovered them," the Judge replied and smiled at Mansfield as she brought him a Seagram's and Seven. He took a drink of it, then took out his handkerchief and wiped his forehead.

Strange, Jake thought, since it's on the cool side in here tonight. Fall had definitely arrived in full force. He made a mental note to adjust the heat accordingly.

"So, Jake, did I tell ya what my kid did last week?" the Judge asked, settling back in his chair. Their conversation shifted to the prowess of the Judge's young son's baseball abilities, and Jake let the Judge change the subject away from the Humphrey story.

A few minutes later, Jake went into the office and adjusted the heat. It wouldn't do to freeze out the customers. Although the Judge had sure been sweating bullets when he told that Humphrey story. Well, you learn something new every day around here, he thought wryly. And it felt good to see the Judge sweat, after he'd made Jake so mad with his advice to leave Kelly alone. Jake still counted the Judge as a friend, but he didn't mind a little payback.

JAKE HAD TO COME UP WITH another way to make some extra money. His reign as Pong machine hustler had run its course. People were wise to the fact that, drunk or sober, he could beat them. Then opportunity came knocking on his door.

Bobby Riggs, a world-famous tennis player, had challenged Billy Jean King, a woman tennis champion, to a match that was being touted as the "Battle of the Sexes." The publicity promoting the event was non-stop. The ads talked about Riggs declaring that any half-decent male player could defeat even the best female players and be guaranteed a victory. Those remarks branded him as a "chauvinist pig" with some groups.

Jake was surprised at the interest the Poodle patrons had in the match. He didn't believe there was a tennis player among them. He played the game and was only average at it, but he had a decent knowledge of the sport and was a big fan.

About two weeks before the big match, Jake took George aside. "This is our chance to clean up. I'm going to take all bets against Billy Jean King. and I suggest you do the same. If you won't take all the action, I'll cover what you won't."

"How can you be so goddamned sure that she's going to win?"

Jake explained, "George, my man, as a former boxer you ought to know that your legs are the first thing to go. He's fifty-five and she's twenty-nine. Need I say more?"

"All right. You sold me, you fucker. I just hope you're right." George walked away, nodding.

Even Pat, after being convinced by Jake, took some action. George stopped at three hundred dollars. He told Jake he had never bet so much on one deal. Jake didn't tell anyone he had bet a total of seven hundred-fifty.

The day finally came. The event was scheduled for Thursday, September 20, 1973, at the Houston Astrodome. The extravaganza was produced with an abundance of fanfare by the ABC Monday Night Football team, with Howard Cosell, in his inimitable style, calling the action, along with commentators Rosie Casals, Gene Scott, and sideline reporter Frank Gifford.

The Poodle was packed; both televisions were on. Jake had added an extra bartender—unusual for a weeknight. The match was scheduled to start at five o'clock, but with all the promotional bullshit, it didn't begin for another twenty minutes, which Jake and Pat both thought was fine, because that just meant selling more booze in the interim. The crowd was boisterous with anticipation, and it sounded like he was at a goddamned football game, Jake thought.

Pat and Jake stood at the bar, surveying the overflowing room and listening to all the men talk about how Riggs was going to kick Billy Jean's ass.

Pat asked, "Jake, why do you have that shit-eating grin on your face?"

"You know, with all the business I'm bringing in tonight, and the money you're going to win, I think I'm entitled to a raise."

Pat seemed at a loss for words. "We . . . we'll talk about it," he finally got out.

Jake watched Pat hustle away, and thought, "Gotcha!"

Shortly before the match, King entered the Astrodome in Cleopatra style, carried aloft in a chair held by four bare-chested muscle men dressed in the style of ancient slaves. The crowd in the Poodle "booed" heartily, then cheered when Riggs entered the dome in a rickshaw drawn by a bevy of scantily-clad models.

Jake whispered to Pat, "Let 'em have their fun, because there'll be a lot of groaning when this evening is over." He grinned as he surveyed the scene.

"I hope to hell you're right," Pat said quietly.

On the TV screens, Jake watched Riggs present King with a giant lollipop, and she gave him a piglet named Larimore Hustle. Jake snorted. This was shaping up to be the Battle of the Sexes that the promoters had dubbed it, but Jake didn't doubt the outcome.

The event finally got underway. Rather than playing her own usual aggressive game, King mostly hugged the baseline, easily handling Rigg's lobs and soft shots, making Riggs cover the entire court as she ran him from side to side.

If Jake had any doubts, they were gone after the middle of the first set. He walked up and down the bar, telling people, "Anybody want to bet more? I'll even give odds." But there were no takers.

After quickly falling behind the baseline, where he had intended to play, Riggs was forced to change to a serve-and-volley game. Even from the net, the result was the same: King defeated him, 6-4, 6-3, 6-3.

At the end of the match, Jake went about collecting from the bitter losers who complained that the match must have been fixed.

He didn't expect to collect everything owed him, but he got most of it.

Pat came up to him. "Thanks for talking me into betting on King, Jake."

Jake looked him in the eye. "You know, Pat, I'm not a gambler. This was a sure thing."

Then a thought hit him. Jesus, what if he'd lost? He'd be up shit creek! He shrugged off that unnecessary worry, smug in his win. It really had been a sure thing, just as he'd told Pat. And it had been the first enjoyable evening he'd had since Dawn's disappearance.

He headed over to George, who started to pour him a drink. Jake held up his hand. "Whoa, partner. That gin is rotting my stomach. This is as good a time as any for me to switch back to my winter drink. Beeeeam and soda," he drew out the name. Jake licked his lips and lit up a cigarette in anticipation.

"Gotcha. Back to Beam and soda." George nodded. "Hey, Jake, if I ever go to Vegas, I'm taking you with me." He poured the drink and set it in front of Jake.

Jake grinned as he toasted George. "You're right, George. Don't ever bet against The Jake."

JAKE WOKE UP WITH A SPLITTING HEADACHE. He looked over and saw a lump in his bed. A blonde, this time. He couldn't remember how she got there or what they did—if anything. He vaguely remembered bringing her home to celebrate all the money he'd won during the tennis match last night. At least he'd managed to allay the guilt he felt over Dawn's death for a few more hours.

He got out of bed and went to take a leak. As he stood in front of the mirror, getting ready to shave, he thought, What a loser I am. He'd been celebrating his win, but Dawn's parents were undoubtedly mourning her loss. And Doyle was still unpunished.

He stared at himself with remorse and disgust. How could he have forgotten about Dawn? And Doyle?

He lathered up his face. His hands shook, and he nicked himself a few times.

"I should have got a fuckin' electric razor," he muttered to his reflection, "but I can never get a close shave with those damn things."

He thought about going to the kitchen and making some coffee, but opted to take a shower first. As the hot water cascaded onto his shoulders, he tried to think of how he could get rid of that bimbo in his bed. He shook his head, not surprised that he couldn't remember her name or how they'd met. He had to get his shit together.

He climbed out of the shower and noticed he was still bleeding from the shaving nicks, so he stuck little dabs of toilet paper on the cuts. He rolled his eyes at the image staring back at him in the mirror. Now he even *looked* like a jerkoff—someone who couldn't handle a goddamned razor.

He put on his robe, walked into the kitchen, started the coffee, and went back into the bedroom.

He shook the sleeping girl, whose back was to him. "Hey, wake up. Wake up. You need to get out of here. I need to leave real soon."

When she rolled over and squinted up at him, he got a better look at her. He stepped back. He really must be a loser, 'cause this broad was no winner.

As JAKE DROVE HOME FROM WORK a week later, he reviewed his progress on his investigation into Doyle's murder of Dawn. He was completely frustrated that he had reached a dead end—just like the police.

HE THOUGHT ABOUT DIFFERENT SCENARIOS where he could entrap Doyle into making the first move against him, which would justify killing that no-good sonofabitch. He had thought about it before but had always dismissed it as fantasy. But now, the idea held serious appeal. "Maybe I could follow him and do a hit and run," Jake mused, but ruled it out because the car would be damaged and they'd trace it back to him—a hit and run wouldn't work. He thought about hiring someone to take out Doyle, but it would probably cost too much money.

He pulled into his driveway. "I have to do something. That asshole can't go free. And I'm sick to death of feeling helpless and guilty."

CHAPTER 18

Monday, October 1

JAKE JUMPED IN HIS MUSTANG and followed Doyle's car to Franklin Avenue and 19th. Doyle pulled into an alley, and Jake followed him in.

Suddenly he couldn't see any lights from the car ahead of him, so he stopped abruptly, exited his car, pulled out his gun, and said to himself, "Now I got the sonofabitch right where I want him."

The problem was that he couldn't see where he was going. Worse, he couldn't see Doyle.

He put his left hand out and felt his way along the alley. He tripped over a garbage can and the sound echoed throughout what felt like half the city.

"Where is that cocksucker?" he swore silently.

Suddenly a white flash burst in the air a few feet ahead of him. It felt like a truck hit him in the chest. He put his left hand up to his jacket and felt warm, wet stickiness.

Two more flashes lit the alley.

"Damn," Jake groaned. "Doyle wins."

The next thing he knew, he was walking around in what appeared to be clouds. He no longer felt any pain, which was confusing.

"What just happened?" he asked no one in particular. "Where the fuck am I?" No one answered; he was very much alone.

He looked around, then down. The clouds parted and he saw a

cemetery. Kelly and the children were there. They were all crying. And there were his mother, his sisters, and his brother. And a few of his old friends.

"*Whose funeral is that?*" *he said aloud. "Why aren't I there with them? Which one of my relatives died?*"

He bent down for a closer look and tried to hear what was being said.

"*Too bad about Jake,*" *his friend Mel Lebewitz said. "He used to be a nice guy. I can't imagine how he ended up like this.*"

Jake woke up sweating.

A FEW HOURS LATER, JAKE PULLED INTO the parking lot of the Poodle. He couldn't shake the dream.

"What a way to go," he thought, pissed that his life had ended too soon in the dream. *Even in my dreams, I have shitty luck.*

He thought about it some more. If his life really did end now . . . it was worthless. He had fuckin' nothing—no Kelly, no kids . . . and to make matters worse, Doyle would have won.

SOON AFTER HE WALKED IN THE DOOR of the Poodle, he recounted the dream to George and to Frank, who was arriving to start his shift.

Frank pinched the bridge of his nose for a moment, then opened his eyes and stared at him. "Jake, I like you, so I'm telling you this for your own good. Do not continue with this investigation of Doyle. He is one dirty, no-good sonofabitch, and no disrespect to you, Jake, but you're in way over your head on this one."

Jake heard what Frank said, but his mind was made up. Nothing Frank could say would stop him from nailing Lucky Doyle. Somebody had to stop Doyle, and since the cops couldn't do it, it was up to him.

George said nothing at the time, but a little later, he called Jake over to the bar and laid it on the line. "Quit fucking around. If you're gonna do something with this guy, my only advice is to get him before he gets you."

Now that made sense. He nodded and smiled wryly at George, "That's the best fuckin' idea you've had since I met you. I'll drink to that." He slapped his hand on the bar and didn't have to wait long before George handed him a Beam and soda.

He hadn't seen hide nor hair of Doyle since Dawn disappeared, and his investigation had stalled. But the guilt over Dawn still ate at him. Jake felt that he would go nuts if he couldn't talk to someone about her. George and Frank just weren't that interested anymore.

He called Kelly. He could count on her to listen.

"Hi, Jake, what's up?" she answered.

He got right to it. "There's something that happened to a young girl who worked here, and I need to talk to someone about it. You're still my best friend, and I'm hoping you'll give me some time . . ."

"Of course I will. This weekend, you have the children. You could come over Saturday night . . . or, come to think of it, why don't I get a sitter, and you and I can go out to dinner."

When Saturday evening finally rolled around and Jake and Kelly went to dinner at The Cork and Cleaver off Highway 12, Jake told Kelly all about Dawn—and a little bit about Doyle.

Kelly was very sympathetic. "That's terrible! And the police told you there's nothing more they can do about it?"

Jake shook his head glumly. "They say that in a murder investigation, if you haven't come up with some leads in the first week or two, then chances are you may never, and the full court press disappears."

Kelly reached across the table, put her hand on Jake's, and squeezed lightly. "Jake, I know you well enough to know you're probably feeling responsible for this in some way."

"Yes, you're right. I promised her father I would look out for her," he replied, choking up a little bit.

"Look, Jake, I'm sure that you did everything that you could. More than most people would."

"But it wasn't enough." He certainly wasn't about to tell her he had his own investigation going. She'd only worry. He gripped her hand tightly.

She patted his hand with her other one. "I'm glad to see your sensitive side, Jake. It seems to have been missing of late."

He gave her a small smile. Christ, if she only knew I was thinking about doing to Doyle, she wouldn't say that, he mused. It felt like getting Doyle would bring the retribution the situation called for, and Jake would finally be able to relax and let go of the guilt.

When he didn't reply, Kelly sighed. "Jake, you can't fool me. I see how broken up and stressed you are."

He nodded. "You know me like a book."

They were quiet for a minute, then Kelly asked, "Was there a funeral? Did you go?"

Jake hung his head. "No, I didn't go. I just couldn't bring myself to."

She smiled sympathetically. "It's okay, Jake." She folded her napkin and put it beside her plate. "Let's go home."

When they arrived, and after the babysitter left, Jake and Kelly went upstairs to her bedroom. He told her, "I'm so tired. I think I'm just going to crap out."

Kelly looked surprised. "Wow, you really must be upset."

About a week later, Doyle turned up at the Poodle. Jake seethed with frustration as he kept his distance and watched Doyle throw down a couple of drinks.

Immediately after that, Doyle got off his stool and walked up to Jake, a threatening look on his face.

Oh, yeah. Here we go, Jake thought. Every muscle in his body was on high alert.

His eyes narrowed, Doyle menacingly ground out, "Back the fuck off. I know what you're up to." He formed the fingers of his right hand in the shape of a gun, aimed it at Jake's face, and pretended to pull the trigger.

Jake was furious. Rage filled him. He could barely control himself—he wanted to punch Doyle right then and there and beat him to a bloody pulp. It was all he could do to keep his arms down at his sides.

George leaped over the bar and planted himself between the two of them. Good thing, Jake thought, because in another second,

I would have reached for my gun. My real gun—not a fuckin' pretend gun, like Doyle just aimed at me.

"Take a fucking hike!" George shot at Doyle.

Doyle roared back, "Get out of my way, or I'll take you down too."

The two men were about the same size, so Jake couldn't see past George, although he could hear him. "Listen up, you mother fucker, or today is going to be your unluckiest day."

Doyle backed off, but he didn't look too happy about it. He glared back and forth between Jake and George, then leveled his hatred-filled gaze at Jake. "I'm not through with you, you little Jew."

Jake's anger exploded. He lunged toward Doyle but George grabbed him and held him back. The front door of the Poodle slammed behind Doyle, and Jake struggled to get free of George so he could rush after Doyle.

Now! Now! I'm gonna take him now. The words pounded in his head. "George, get out of my way, let me finish him now. Now!"

George swung him around, and stuck his face in front of Jake's. Jake blinked and finally focused on what George was saying.

"Listen to me. Listen to me!" George shook him. "You don't stand a fucking chance against that guy! And I don't want to be put in this position again, do you understand me?"

Jake took a deep breath. "All right, man, you're right," he said, and the bitch of it was that George really was right—for now. Jake would lose in a fistfight with Doyle—and lose badly.

Jake promised himself, however, that he would take Doyle down somehow—or he'd die trying.

CHAPTER 19

Saturday, October 13

THE CONFRONTATION WITH DOYLE continued to weigh heavily on his mind, but he knew he couldn't do anything about it at the moment—not until another opportunity presented itself. He did, however, enjoy fantasizing about the various ways he could kill Doyle and get away with it.

The Poodle was nearly empty tonight and Jake picked up on a conversation between two customers, neither of whom would qualify as a Rhodes scholar.

"Those fucking Jews and Arabs fighting each other. Why should we care? That's all the news covers these days. I say let them kill each other and be done with it."

Jake's back got up as he listened to them talking about the Israeli-Arab War. He was about to smack them when the other one said, "Thanks to that war, it took me twice as much money to fill up my gas tank this week as it did last week."

Jake took a deep breath and reined in his temper when he realized they weren't bad-mouthing the Jews so much as bitching about the price of gas, which had more than doubled since the war started. He couldn't completely disagree with them about the gas prices.

His attention shifted as he heard George tell a drunk-looking guy that he was cut off. "You need to leave," George told the man, who had sandy-colored hair and a thin build. Jake walked over to escort the man out.

When Jake was a few feet away, the guy suddenly turned and took a swing at him. Fortunately, Jake sidestepped the punch and hit him with a solid right.

The guy went down hard, bleeding from his nose, where Jake had struck him.

"Now, are you going to leave?" Jake asked impatiently. He'd had more than enough stupid people for one day.

The man, who was about Jake's own age, picked himself up. "I know what this is about. You're prejudiced against Indians, aren't you?" he said as he staggered backward a few feet.

Bemused, Jake asked, "What are you talking about?" The man had blue eyes and a fair complexion. He certainly didn't look like any Indians Jake had ever seen. Jake kept his fists clenched, ready to hit the guy again if needed.

The man told Jake, "I'm part Indian," and stood up straight, despite the blood running down his face.

Jake laughed, "Which part?"

Still a bit wobbly on his feet, the man explained that his great uncle was of the Chippewa tribe from northern Minnesota.

Jake couldn't keep a straight face. "Well, if you're an Indian, then where's your feather?"

The man glared at him but didn't rise to the bait.

Some of the regulars had been following the conversation. They chimed in, making Indian noises by slapping their mouths and jumping up and down.

Jake was still laughing, but he figured enough was enough. The guy had had his fifteen seconds of fame.

Jake took a step toward him, but the guy backed off and hustled toward the door. As he was leaving, he turned his head and yelled, "You haven't heard the last of this!"

The next evening, Jake found out that the stupid prick wasn't kidding. Trouble always seemed to come in bunches. At least that's the way Jake saw it. On several occasions during his months at the Poodle, he'd said to himself—or anyone else who would listen—"Now I've seen everything" . . . only to quickly discover just how wrong he had been.

Lost in thought about Doyle, he didn't notice two disheveled, dark-haired men entering the bar. When he did, Nick had already served them drinks; George was occupied at the far end of the bar. Since it was Saturday and they were busy, both nighttime bartenders were on duty.

Jake's attention remained on the two customers, who were clearly Indians. They looked like shit: dark, pocked-marked faces, dirty hair, and filthy clothes. They reminded Jake of when he worked part-time in college as a helper on a milk truck. The Indians would be standing in line, suffering from the shakes, as they stood outside of Danny's Bar, waiting for it to open at seven in the morning.

It didn't dawn on Jake until two more Indians walked in that this was about last night. There were no more open seats at the bar so the two new guys asked their buddies to order for them. George was right there, and Jake knew he could sense trouble brewing. He and Jake gave each other the high sign.

Before Jake or George took more than a step toward the Indians, one of the local rabble rousers exacerbated the situation when he said in a loud voice, making sure everyone could hear, "So, the Lone Ranger and Tonto are surrounded by Indians. The Lone Ranger says to Tonto, 'What are we going to do?' Tonto replies, 'What's this *we* shit, white man?'" The crowd roared.

Another regular chimed in, "What do you call a queer Indian?" He paused. "A brave sucker!"

The place was into it now and jokes were flying.

Jake moved to the end of the bar, reached under it, and grabbed his club. He tucked his tie into his shirt front because he didn't want anyone using it to pull him down. He was ready.

Three more Indians arrived, bringing the count to seven. They immediately joined their friends, and tried to push their way up to the crowded bar.

Someone in the crowd of regulars yelled, "How do you keep Indians out of your back yard? Move the trash cans to the front!"

Even Jake had a hard time not laughing out loud on that one, but he kept his face serious as he stared at the group at the bar.

The Indians seemed oblivious to the jokes. They were intent on getting a drink. Just as Nick was about to take their orders, George shoved him aside, and grabbed the half-empty glasses from the original two Indians at the bar. He glared at them, and the tooth-pick between his lips barely moved. "I'm gonna tell you fuckin' Indians how it's going to be. You're gone."

One of them stood up and took a swing at George. Big mistake, Jake chuckled as he rushed to that end of the bar.

George easily deflected the blow and threw a vicious right, knocking the man and his bar stool to the floor.

The front door opened and a few more Indians rushed in to join their friends. Jake counted about ten of them now.

Pushing and shoving erupted in that part of the bar. And then the punching started.

Other than George, Jake didn't know who threw the next punch that actually connected, but it hardly mattered. A fight was on! Ten Indians against everyone else.

Unfortunately, Jake couldn't get through the crowd of regulars to hit one of the Indians, so he climbed up onto the bar.

At the same time, George leaped over the bar to join the fray.

Once he stood on top of the bar and had a decent view of the worsening situation, Jake figured that he could be the most effective by staying there. He could more easily identify the enemy and take him out, which he proceeded to do, grinning. As he ran down the length of the bar and headed back in the other direction, he noticed that two of the waitresses were stationed at either end of the dining room with bar stools to fend off anyone from getting into the dining area. Using his club, Jake knew he had connected with a few heads and hoped he hadn't hit any of the good guys. He got carried away and thought of the James Cagney movie, *White Heat*. Jake yelled, "Made it, Ma! Top of the world!"

George called out, "Jake, watch out, for Christ sakes. You almost got me!"

Supercharged by now, Jake—in some perverse way—was enjoying this donnybrook.

One of the Indians tried to climb onto the bar, but Jake kicked him in the head. The guy disappeared in the mass of bodies below.

He hoped that someone had had the good sense to call the cops by now. While it was cathartic to swing his club at the rabble-rousing Indians, the situation was already out of hand.

The front door flew open and two very large German shepherds—barking and growling—entered on leashes held by police wearing riot gear. The dogs' presence immediately diffused the fighting crowd.

Before the cops could ask, Jake yelled to them, "I'm the manager! Don't shoot me."

Jake stayed where he was—on top of the bar—as he watched the German shepherds leap and tug against their restraints. Medics arrived on the heels of the riot gear cops, and treated the wounded. Seven out of ten of the Indians had to be hospitalized, and several of them had concussions and an assortment of broken bones and bruises.

He couldn't decide if he felt good that the problem had ended, or disappointed that it wouldn't continue.

As soon as the cops and the vicious dogs left, Jake yelled, "Drinks on the house!" and climbed down off the bar.

He was glad he'd thought of calming everyone down with free alcohol, because a cheer went up after his announcement. One of the local hoods who had participated in the fight said, "Jake, you are one crazy mother fucker! And we love you."

Someone else said, "Three cheers for The Jake," and so it went. The general feeling had been that the patrons who had participated had enjoyed themselves.

He felt like he'd just won the heavyweight championship. George's toothpick was still ensconced in his mouth, and all was well. By closing time, Jake was so drunk he could barely walk. George helped him close up and took him over to the Anthony, where he got him a room to sleep it off again.

Jake awoke about ten-thirty the next morning. His head was splitting, and he had the shakes. His mouth was dry, and he needed a drink.

He closed his eyes in disgust. "Really? I need a drink? That's my first thought?" he asked himself. Yes, he answered, and I need a fucking drink bad.

He snuck out of the hotel, raced across the street, and hoped that Pat hadn't seen him. He dashed into Jimmy's Broiler, where he ordered a big breakfast and coffee. He was always hungry when he was hung over. The waitress kept his coffee cup full.

After he'd consumed his bacon, eggs, hash browns, pancakes, and about six cups of coffee, he checked his watch.

Shit. It was nearly noon. He hurried to his car and drove home. Well, not home, per se, he snorted. Not his real home, not the one with Kelly and the kids, but the house he shared with Pete.

As he turned off of Hennepin Avenue and drove onto Wayzata Boulevard, he took stock of his life. It seemed like a good time—hung over, tired, needing a shower, and missing his wife. No, it was too painful to think about Kelly. Instead, his thoughts shifted to his job at the Poodle. Despite last night's entertainment, he was getting sick and tired of babysitting the dysfunctional masses and cleaning up their messes.

So what was he qualified to do? He liked some aspects of the restaurant business, but not the violence of the Poodle. Actually, he probably enjoyed the violence too much, now that he thought about it. He needed to get out of there and do something different with his life.

After I deal with Doyle, of course, he promised himself.

If there was ever going to be a chance to get back with Kelly and the kids, he would need a daytime job so he could resume a normal life.

He glanced at the speedometer to make sure he wasn't exceeding the speed limit. He undoubtedly still had enough alcohol in him that he wouldn't pass any type of test if they pulled him over. Damn good thing Kelly couldn't see him now.

He checked the want ads when he got home. Nothing. Squat.

THAT FOLLOWING SATURDAY EVENING, Kelly came in the back door of the Poodle about six o'clock, found Jake, and told him, "Thanks for letting me park here." She was going to a rock concert. Some group called Cheap Trick. The concert was at Sam's, an old, art deco-style bus depot that had been converted into an auditorium. It was only three blocks away from the Poodle.

Damn, Kelly looked good tonight. Her hair was down and loose, just like he liked it, and her short skirt showed off her long legs. Jake's stomach clenched when he thought about what could happen to her at a crowded rock concert.

"You be very careful of all those young punks," he warned.

"Not to worry. I'll be with my friend, Barbara. However, I really do appreciate your concern, Jake."

Jake reluctantly said good-bye and asked her to come through the Poodle on the way back to her car later that night, so he would know that she was safe.

God, she is beautiful, he thought as he watched her walk out the front door. He sighed and went about the business of running the asylum.

Not much happened that evening. He kept looking at the clock, anxiously awaiting Kelly's return. She came back around midnight.

Kelly told him about the concert, and he feigned interest. He'd never heard of the group and couldn't understand why anyone would listen to that shit. But Kelly had obviously had a good time.

Out of the corner of his eye, he noticed Doyle come in and sit at the other end of the bar. Jake's gut tightened, especially when he noticed Doyle eyeing Kelly with what Jake interpreted as an *aha!* look of glee. The asshole looked delighted to see Jake with Kelly.

This is not good, he thought, glancing between Kelly and the watchful Doyle. He had to get her out of there.

Jake took her by the arm and hurried her out the back door and into her car parked in the alley. "Be sure to call me when you get home," he asked. She agreed and waved good-bye.

Jake went back into the bar and noticed that Lucky had left. Pissed that he'd missed an opportunity to get in Doyle's face and provoke him into doing something, he asked George, "Why do you serve that asshole Doyle, anyway?"

George shrugged. "Listen, as long as he pays for his drinks and behaves himself, he's just like any other asshole that comes in here."

Shit. Did nobody take Doyle seriously? He was a menace to society and didn't deserve to be walking the streets, let alone be served drinks at the Poodle.

Jake went into the office to get some paperwork done, still regretting that he hadn't been able to egg Doyle on and perhaps incite him to take a swing at Jake—or reach for a knife or a gun. Jake relished the idea of Doyle coming after him.

Kelly called twenty minutes later. "Jake, I think someone followed me home."

Jake didn't ask if she was sure. Kelly wasn't prone to exaggeration. If she said someone followed her, it must be so. "Make sure all the doors are locked. I will have my bouncer, Frank, who is a policeman, call the St. Paul cops and have them patrol the house until I get there in a few minutes."

He rushed back into the bar and told Frank about it, and gave him the address of the house. Frank called the St. Paul cops right away and made the arrangements. "It's handled, Jake," Frank said. "They will send a patrol to cruise the neighborhood and drive by every few minutes."

Jake was beside himself. He was stuck here at the Poodle for another hour, at least. He knocked back a couple of drinks to fortify himself. Fuck that, he thought, and then asked George to close up the bar for him so that he could get over to Kelly's house immediately.

He didn't allow the dark thought that had been nagging at him to fully form in his mind until he was actually driving on the road, racing over to Kelly's. If he caught the son of a bitch, he would definitely kill him. There was no doubt in his mind that Doyle had left the Poodle and followed Kelly home.

Jake drove over the Lake Street Bridge, turned right onto Exeter Place, went past the house, and turned into the alley in the back. He leaped out of the car, drew his .357, and started toward the house.

Suddenly he was blinded by extremely bright lights.

Someone yelled, "Throw down your weapon and lay on the ground, face down."

Oh fuck, Jake thought, it's the cops and they're going to kill me. He shouted back, "Don't shoot! I'm the guy that called you."

They surrounded him and took his wallet out of his back pocket and found his driver's license and gun permit.

Just then, Kelly came out of the house and said, "It's okay. He's my husband."

After a few minutes of apologies and thanks back and forth, the cops left.

Jake followed Kelly into the house. Amazingly, the children had slept through all the commotion.

Kelly said," You stink like the bar. Go take a shower and then come to bed."

Well, if you insist, he grinned to himself.

Sometime later, while they were in bed and after they had made love, Jake said, "You called me your husband."

Kelly replied, "Don't let it go to your head. I just didn't want you killed." She leaned over and kissed him good night.

Jake thought about how close he'd come to getting shot by the cops. Then he smiled. Ah, it was worth it!

Jake awoke at eight o'clock. Kelly was still sleeping.

He thought about last night as he watched her and played with a strand of her hair. He had almost been killed but what a way to end the evening! He picked up another strand and watched it glow in the morning light peeking through the drapes. The more he was with her, the more he thought that maybe she wanted a future with him.

Kelly stirred; Jake leaned over and kissed her on the lips.

Kelly murmured, "What?"

"How about an encore?"

She smiled. "Just don't wake the children."

At eight-thirty, Sarah and Sean ran into the room and jumped on the bed, delighted to see their mother and father together.

CHAPTER 20

Sunday, October 21

THE NEXT NIGHT, JAKE TALKED TO A FEW OF THE HOODS that came in the Poodle, and asked them where he could find Doyle, where the asshole was hanging out these days.

Nobody seemed to know anything. He went around talking to everyone—especially the women whose names Jose had given him—but with no luck. No one had seen Doyle.

During his shifts at the Poodle, Jake continued to bug anyone who would possibly know anything about Doyle or what he was up to lately or where to find him. He still didn't have any evidence or witnesses who were willing to talk. Even worse, Doyle had seen him with Kelly and had likely followed her home. Now, it was getting personal, and Jake wasn't about to stand by and do nothing while Doyle threatened his family.

When Jimmy Box came in, Jake asked him the same questions.

Jimmy replied, "Doyle's gone to ground because he said there was too much heat from the fuzz."

Shit. "Thanks, Jimmy, but if you hear anything, I'd really appreciate knowing."

"No problem. But in case you didn't know it, the Old Man is still fuckin' with my scotch."

Jake laughed. "Jimmy, some things never change," he said and walked away.

Jake signaled George for a drink and thought about Jimmy's news about Doyle. He was frustrated and beside himself. How was he going to get that sonofabitch if he'd gone to ground? His stomach churned. He downed the rest of his drink.

"George," he called, his arms raised and out to the side, "bring me more, bring me several more drinks." Fuck. Now what? He pondered his next step . . . and couldn't think of anything.

JAKE GOT OFF HIS HORSE *and tied it to the railing. He had been riding for a long time and had worked up a mighty thirst. After brushing himself off, he walked through the swinging doors into the Last Chance Saloon.*

Jake went directly to the bar and said in a loud voice, "Whiskey. And leave the bottle."

The bartender nodded. He had a crew cut, and a toothpick in his mouth. Something about him looked familiar. Jake asked, "Don't I know you from somewhere? What's your name?"

"The name's George," the man replied impatiently as he slid the bottle and shot glass across the bar to Jake, "and I ain't never seen you before." He walked away.

Jake downed a couple of shots and looked around the room. Several other customers looked familiar but he just couldn't place them.

He glanced around again. He had arranged to meet his girl Kelly here, and she'd promised she'd come, despite her dislike of meeting in a saloon.

He didn't see her. He checked his pocket watch. She was more than an hour overdue. Worry raced through him.

He grabbed the arm of one of the barmaids and asked her if she had seen Kelly.

"Hey, let go," the girl said in a loud voice. "You're hurting me!"

Jake was tired and short on patience. He let go of the girl's arm but growled, "Tell me where the fuck she is." He briefly described Kelly.

A man next to him said, "I saw a girl of that description go upstairs—unwillingly—with one bad hombre—Lucky Doyle. And if you know what's good for you, you won't go up there. The man's a cold-blooded killer."

Jake lunged for the stairs, climbed halfway, and suddenly stopped. He heard nothing; it was deathly quiet behind him. No talking, no piano playing. He whirled around. Everyone was looking up at him.

"Jake! Jake, help me," he heard Kelly cry out.

He drew his gun and continued up the stairs. "Kelly! Kelly, where are you?"

"Jake!"

He rushed to the door of the room where her voice was coming from.

He heard shots and looked down to see blood coming out of his chest. Kelly screamed.

He woke up.

HE WAS STILL RATTLED WHEN HE WENT TO WORK that evening. Late in his shift, he stood at the bar, drinking his usual, and allowed himself to think about this most recent nightmare.

Why am I having these dreams, Doctor? he asked himself. He pulled another cigarette out of the pack of Winstons, and lit it.

A voice in his head replied, "Dummy, they're trying to tell you something."

"Yeah, yeah, I get it." He stubbed out his half-smoked cigarette. "Someone's gonna shoot me. Lucky Doyle, probably, but it could be anyone."

He kept picturing himself getting shot, over and over. Fear gripped him and a kind of paranoia took over. He looked around the bar and wondered who from the crowd would be the one to shoot him?

Jake kept drinking, steadily, hoping to quell the images in his head and the unnerving feeling that his dreams were actually prophesies.

A few drinks later, the paranoia had worsened. Death stared him in the face. He had to do something to stop it, to shut it up, to get a handle on it, so he went up and down the bar, asking customers, "Are you the one? Are you the one?"

A customer yelled, "Hey, George! Get the straitjacket. Jake's finally gone over the edge!"

When he heard that, Jake shook his head, trying to clear it and realized he'd been acting like a neurotic, drunken fool.

"I gotta get out of this place," he muttered to himself for the umpteenth time.

THE NEXT MORNING JAKE WOKE UP in a strange bed. It took him a while to realize he was in a room at the Anthony—and alone again. In addition to his head pounding, it felt like someone had dropped an anvil on it. His stomach was tied up in knots, and his hands shook. He laid in bed, full of disgust and self-recrimination.

Fuck. He'd gone round the bend. He'd lost control—waking up in the Anthony and not even remembering how he got there. The last thing he did remember was nearly passing out at the Poodle last night, after accusing people of being the one who'll shoot him.

I don't even recognize myself, he thought in a wave of self-loathing, mortified at his behavior last night. He really had become more of Mr. Hyde than the good Dr. Jekyll. Kelly was right—the lines were blurring.

The drinking, the violence, the smoking—he was up to more than two packs a day now—was all escalating, forcing him into a downward spiral that could only end in disaster. He thought about how many fights he'd been in lately—ones that months ago he would have avoided. His temper was frayed, perhaps beyond repair. Shit, what if he lost his temper with Kelly, God forbid? He shuddered and his stomach heaved.

How much longer could he hide this from Kelly and the kids? How much longer could he keep doing this? He was losing the battle, losing control.

Fuck.

CHAPTER 21

Thursday, November 1

JAKE HAD BEEN PROCRASTINATING about looking for a job for months. He had haphazardly looked in the want ads in recent weeks but without any real effort. However, his last conversation with Kelly convinced him he'd have to do more than think about it.

When he'd told her that he thought it was Doyle who had followed her, and that she needed to be careful—and why—she was furious.

"Do you even know the difference between you and the people you talk about there? Look at the trouble you've caused, Jake! I'm supposed to go around looking over my shoulder because some crazy person is after me because of *you*? Promise me that you're going to get out of there, Jake, if not for your sake, then for mine and the children's."

Days later, he still felt terrible about the danger Kelly was in. And he was still worried. Just because Doyle went to ground didn't mean the scumbag wasn't up to something—or would surface again. And what form would that take—what kind of danger lie ahead for Kelly, or the children, or him?

He leaned against the bar and sipped his Jim Beam. Was this number six for the evening? It hardly mattered. Nothing took the edge off the worry and fear for Kelly.

He had made up his mind that he really was going to find another job. No more dicking around. The longer he worked for the Poodle, the more likely something really bad would happen to him or his family.

Today when he'd checked the want ads, he finally saw an ad that intrigued him.

The new Investor Diversified Building had been completed. It housed two restaurants and a bar on the fiftieth floor. They were looking for a few managers, day and night time. If he could work days, he could spend more time with his children and maybe if he wasn't too far gone, get back to a normal life. Even get back together with Kelly. The ad said to mail in a résumé and if they were interested they would call for an interview.

He ground out his cigarette. What a joke. The only hospitality experience he had was the Poodle! Who was he kidding. They would never hire him. They would probably have a good laugh and send him one of those standard form rejection letters.

Fuck it! He would spend some time and create a decent résumé showing his ten years of other management experience. And he would write a cover letter that would knock their socks off.

Jake hoped it was not wishful thinking and that he really would have a chance. He planned his strategy.

He couldn't work on his résumé while he was at the Poodle—someone might see—but he could start on it tomorrow, before work, and have at least a couple of hours to write the damn thing, and the cover letter too. He could mail it on his way to work.

His decision made, he ordered another drink to seal the deal with himself.

THIS TIME, HE ACTUALLY FOLLOWED THROUGH ON HIS PLAN. When he tipped the envelope with the résumé and cover letter into the mailbox, he sent a short, fervent plea heavenward that this would be a new beginning, a rebirth of sorts. But he still had some unfinished business to take care of at the Poodle.

Doyle.

SUNDAY MORNING, JAKE RETURNED THE CHILDREN to Kelly's after having them stay with him overnight.

Sean yelled, "Mom, we're home."

Kelly responded, "I'm upstairs, just got out of the shower."

Jake went up the stairs, not wanting to miss seeing Kelly naked. She had a towel wrapped around her. He moved to embrace her, but she gently pushed him away.

That's when he noticed a nasty bruise on her arm. "What happened?"

"Oh, it's nothing," she replied and looked away.

"Bullshit, let me have a closer look. That looks real sore. How'd you get it?"

"Well, if you must know, the guy I have been seeing . . . we had an argument and he grabbed me and-and . . . you see the results. I won't be seeing him again. No big deal."

Jake felt like his head was going to explode with anger, but he tried to contain himself. He didn't want Kelly to think he was over-reacting. He took a deep breath and asked, "You mean that Brian Gold guy I met a few weeks back?"

"No, no," she replied, "Gary Nelson is his name. Anyway, as I told you, I won't be seeing him again."

Jake narrowed his gaze on the bright purple marks on her fore-arm and thought, Kelly, my dear, you may not be seeing him, but I sure will.

He pretended to let the whole thing go, and went downstairs. He waited for Kelly to come downstairs and then said he had to go upstairs to use the toilet.

Instead, he went quietly into her bedroom and located her address book. He found Nelson's address on some letters the jerk had written her. He memorized the address. It was on 27th and Girard Avenue South, a couple miles south of downtown. He said his good-byes to Kelly and the children soon after that, and went to work.

Driving downtown, Jake said to himself, "Oh, shit, I'll have to wait until Saturday to deal with this, when the guy likely won't be working. I'm gonna pay this guy Nelson a visit—a visit he will never forget. I'll go in the morning, before he has time to get on with his *last* day."

That night he told George the story and what he was planning to do about it. George asked him if he wanted him to come along for back up.

"No thanks. I'll do this one by myself."

George replied, "Okay, but do yourself a favor. Do *not* bring your gun with you."

Jake nodded, as if in agreement, but he thought, "I'm bringing that fucking gun, no doubt about it."

Jake could hardly contain himself until Saturday. He was so upset that thoughts of Doyle barely came to mind all week.

At nine o'clock that morning, he approached Nelson's residence in an older apartment building. He hoped to catch him before he went out. He checked the mailboxes and found out Nelson lived on the second floor. He climbed the wooden stairs and paused before knocking on the right door.

He took a deep breath. He had tried very hard all week and especially this morning to control his emotions. He thought, "Okay, I have them under control. I can remain calm."

He knocked.

A guy in pajamas opened the door without even asking who it was

Jake exploded into the room, smashing Nelson in the face with a solid right. He fell down and Jake kicked him in the ribs. Then Jake jumped on him and hit him, first with a left, then a right, and then he repeated the sequence—several times.

Blood gushed out of Nelson's nose and above his left eye.

When Jake was satisfied that there would be no resistance, he paused to catch his breath.

Terror and confusion filled Nelson's eyes. He gasped for air, trying to speak, but nothing came out.

Jake pulled out the .357 Magnum and pushed it against Nelson's right eye. Jake almost felt sorry for the poor slob, but he had to finish what he started.

"Listen very carefully to what I am saying. I could kill you right now, do you believe me?"

Nelson nodded once, jerkily, and his eyes blinked as his gaze shifted from Jake to the gun and back again.

"Okay, Nelson, you little shit. You are never to call, write, or in any way attempt to contact Kelly Sherman. Are we clear?"

Another tight nod from Nelson.

Jake holstered his gun, stood up, and became aware of a foul smell. The little prick had just shit in his pajamas.

Jake left the apartment, not sure how he felt about what had just happened. He sighed as he got in the Mustang and slammed the door. On the one hand, he had defended his wife's honor. On the other hand, he had just come close to killing someone.

THE TELEPHONE RANG and Jake woke up with a start.

He looked at the clock. Nine a.m. Who would be calling him at this god-awful hour?

He leaped out of bed to catch the phone before it stopped ringing. It could be an emergency with Kelly and the kids, he thought as he ran naked through the house to the kitchen. An emergency made the most sense to him, because everyone else would know not to call him that early.

He grabbed the phone. "Hello?"

"May I speak to Jake Sherman, please?"

He cleared his throat, then shook his head, trying to be alert. "This is Jake."

"This is Nels Tendt calling from the Orion Room at the IDS Tower. How are you today?"

Jake was surprised, but pleased. "I'm fine," he said with a smile. "Yes, Mr. Tendt?"

"The reason I'm calling is we received your résumé and we would like you to come in for an interview for a restaurant management position."

Jake silently yelled, Yes, yes!

Tendt continued, "Would Friday at 2 o'clock work for you?"

Hell, Tendt could have told him to be there at two in the morning and he would! Instead, he replied, "Yes, that would be perfect."

"Good. Go to the security desk in the lobby and they will have your name and will tell you where to go," Tendt explained.

"Thank you, and I'm looking forward to meeting you." They said good-bye and Jake hung up. He stared at the phone.

He wanted to call Kelly, but she was at work, he thought as he glanced at the clock on the stove.

"Well, so, if not Kelly, then who else?" he asked himself.

He looked out the window at the gray, rainy day and realized, sadly, there wasn't anyone else he wanted to share this good news with.

He shoved aside his bleak thoughts and congratulated himself on getting an interview. *Damn, I'm good.*

He had an extra bounce in his step as he made himself a cup of coffee, then jumped in the shower and shaved.

He paused as he dried himself off. What was he doing? Christ, he had six hours before he needed to be at work. He was too wide awake to go back to bed so he finished getting ready. Then he decided that he wanted to be prepared well in advance, so he walked to the closet and grabbed his favorite navy-blue suit to take to the cleaners. He also made sure he had a clean white shirt. He got out his good pair of black oxfords and polished them.

An ugly thought came to mind. *Oh, shit, I hope I don't get in a fight before Friday. That's all I need, is to walk in with a black eye . . . or another cast.*

His shoes polished and his suit in a bag, he left the house a couple of hours early. After extracting a promise from the dry cleaners that his suit would be ready on Thursday, he headed downtown to his regular barber shop in the basement of the Dyckman Hotel.

After crossing that errand off his list, he drove to the Poodle. Even if he was early, there was always plenty to do there. With the interview on Friday and the very real possibility of a new job ahead of him, he was all the more eager to get Doyle.

Jake walked the block of Hennepin Avenue between the parking lot and the Poodle and admired the sunshine peeking through the clouds. The leaves were off the trees, but no sign of snow yet.

When Jake walked into the Poodle, he noticed the Old Man and the Dragon Lady having a late lunch. Pat was shooting the shit with customers at the bar. He paused to rib Jake. "Can't stay away from the place, can you? Your home away from home?"

Jake smiled and headed toward the office. Nothing could deter his good mood.

Pat nodded a good-bye at the customer he had been talking with, then caught up to Jake. "Actually, Jake, I'm glad you're here. My dad and I want to talk to you about something."

Jake's steps had slowed and now he turned around to face Pat. Oh, shit. How could they already know he was looking for a different job? Now they would going to fire his ass.

Pat signaled to his father and the three of them headed into the restaurant and sat down at a corner table. The waitress brought coffee for everyone.

Jake was resigned. The other shoe was about to drop. Could he deny job-hunting, or the upcoming interview? His brain worked furiously, trying to come up with excuses for whatever accusations they were about to throw his way.

While the Old Man dumped sugar in his coffee, Pat said to Jake, "You know, you've been with us almost a year. My dad and I are really pleased with the way you've gained control of our place *and* of the customers. Even though you think there are a lot of problems, it's a lot less than it used to be. Plus, the majority of the customers like you. Can you believe it?" he smiled.

Jake straightened up. Whew! He had dodged another bullet. He relaxed, lit a cigarette, and exhaled away from the two men because neither of them smoked.

Carl chimed in, "My only criticism is that you get all the nice ass around here."

Jake leaned forward. "Carl, there's ass, and then there's good ass, and there ain't no good ass here at the Poodle."

They all had a good laugh at that.

"Seriously," Pat said, "we're going to give you a nice raise."

Jake was suddenly very confident. The situation looked better and better. "How nice of a raise?"

"How does twenty percent suit you?"

"It suits me very well, Pat," Jake smiled, and decided a little bullshit would be appropriate now. "I want to compliment you guys in that you've been very fair and easy to work for."

Both men nodded their thanks. Pat asked, "So, do you have any concerns or questions, Jake?"

Jake sat back and offered, sarcastically, "The only gripe I have is that you guys don't carry any hazard insurance." That got a chuckle out of everyone.

Pat leaned back in his chair. "Well, do you want to order some lunch now, Jake?"

"Sure," he said, but thought, What I'd really like now is a double Beam and soda.

He ordered first and while the other two men took their turns, Jake sat lost in thought. If he got the IDS job, it wouldn't happen until the first of the year. But now, with this extra money from his raise, he could really go all out for Christmas for Kelly and the kids.

Isn't this the shits, he thought ruefully. They're giving me a raise, and I'm applying for another job.

FRIDAY NIGHT, JAKE WAITED FOR THE RIGHT TIME to go into the Poodle's office and call Kelly. He couldn't wait to tell her about the interview he'd had that day, with the hope that she'd be excited for him. Getting her approval was still important to him. Also, it would show her that he wasn't procrastinating anymore.

He dialed the phone and she answered. He hadn't told her yet that he'd applied for the job, so this was all news to her.

The words tumbled out of his mouth almost as fast as he could think them. "It's going to be the tallest building west of the Mississippi, it's going to open sometime in January, and they're looking for managers for their restaurants and bar on the fiftieth floor. It'll be an opportunity for me to get the hell out of this dump and work for a first-rate facility. I told them the job I was interested in was that of a daytime manager."

He leaned forward in his seat. "Kelly, if I get this job, I'll be able to be more of a husband and a father than I was before."

She was silent for a moment, then replied, "Jake, I sincerely hope you get the job, but . . . I don't want to beat a dead horse, but we won't be getting back together."

Jake's bubble burst. His shoulders sagged and his breath caught in his throat. Deep down, he knew that if he looked at things realistically, there was no chance with Kelly. She was right. He hung up the phone without saying good-bye.

Dejected, he went to the bar and, as was his answer to everything, he ordered the usual.

ON THURSDAY NIGHT, JAKE MADE HIS ROUNDS, walking up and down the bar, buying drinks, and exchanging meaningless chatter with customers.

Just another day at the office, he thought as he paused and lit a cigarette. He thought about the IDS interview he'd had almost two weeks ago. He was anxious and concerned because he hadn't been called back for a second interview yet. He decided that if he didn't hear from them next week, he would call them. He'd told Pete that he might be getting a call from someone about the job, in case they called in the evening when Pete was there and Jake was at work. During the day, Jake had stayed home and close to the phone, so he didn't think he'd missed their call.

The door to the Poodle opened and a cold gust of wind blew in, along with Jimmy Box.

Jimmy was the epitome of "what you see is what you get," and Jake liked him, despite the guy's background—murdering some black dude in the back and getting away with self-defense, thanks to Box's attorney, Ron Meshbesher. Jake had known Meshbesher's brother, Kenny, back in high school. Both Kenny and his brother Ron had become attorneys. Good ones, apparently.

Jake greeted Jimmy. "What's new, my man?"

"Same old, same old," Jimmy responded as he took a seat at the bar. He ordered a J&B from George, warning him, "The old man is still marrying that fucking cheap scotch to my J&B, so don't give me any of that crap he's mixed."

Jake laughed, "I've given up on that one, Jimmy."

George shrugged his shoulders, his toothpick intact, and passed Jimmy his drink.

Jake leaned on the bar next to Jimmy and lit up a cigarette, then told George, "Bring me my regular." He settled in and turned to Jimmy. He knew Jimmy would always have the latest gossip as to what was going on on the Avenue. Jake had heard part of a story but not all of it. Jimmy would have the full account. "What's this I hear about your friend, Bill?"

"Yeah, that dummy got caught robbing a fucking liquor store. He's going away for a loooong time." Jimmy swallowed half his drink in one gulp. "Oh, by the way, I saw your buddy Doyle the other night at the Magic Bar."

Jake's reaction was immediate. Gotcha! he thought as he straightened. *You're a dead man, Doyle.*

It figured, though, that the bar that Doyle surfaced at would be way out of the downtown area and therefore out of Jake's comfort zone. He probably wouldn't know anyone who worked there, despite the fact that the Magic Bar catered to the same type of clientele the Poodle did. But now that Doyle had surfaced, it was only a matter of time, Jake thought, and Doyle would be his.

He lowered his voice and said, "Jimmy, when you see that mother fucker again, tell him The Jake is looking for him."

Jimmy leaned back, his eyes wide, and said, "I'll pass on the message, but are you sure? I hope you know what you're doing, man."

Jake nodded once. Hell, yes, he knew what he was doing.

"Have a nice night, Jimmy," he replied, then walked to the far end of the bar where George was so he could order another Beam.

George said, "You look really pissed off, Jake. You didn't get into an argument with Jimmy, did ya?"

Jake started to answer, then decided not to tell George about Doyle. He didn't want another lecture. Instead, he answered, "No, no, man. We didn't have any argument. I'm just thinking about other things."

As he sipped his drink, he fantasized that Doyle would come looking for him, then—BANG! BANG!—he would kill Doyle and it would be in self-defense. Justice would be served. An eye for an eye.

With a satisfied sigh, he set his empty glass on the counter and beckoned George.

George took a few seconds to pour Jake another drink, then walked over to him. "Now you've got a shit-eating grin on your face. You look like the fucking cat that just swallowed the fucking canary."

"That I am, George. That I am."

CHAPTER 22

Thursday, December 13

JAKE DROPPED FOUR QUARTERS INTO THE SLOT on the cigarette machine and pulled the lever. A pack of Winstons dropped into his waiting hand.

In spite of all his efforts to not think about it, he always came back to the same thing: How could he get to Doyle before Doyle got to him?

Suddenly he heard a loud crash and a thud. He looked to where the sound had come from.

Oh, shit.

A huge man had fallen off his bar stool and was lying on the floor, and the overturned stool was careening into a nearby table and chairs. The man didn't get up. For that matter, he didn't even move.

Jake hurried over and felt the man's neck for his pulse. The guy was so fat that Jake had to push hard to find it. He didn't, so he felt around in several other places on the guy's neck. No luck.

George hurried over. "How bad is it?"

Jake stood up, his hands on his hips. "You aren't going to believe this, but this fucker is dead. Dead, dead, dead."

They both stared down at the enormous man. He was a white guy, although now he looked rather gray. Dressed in a dark suit and tie, the man must have to have all his clothes custom made, Jake figured, and the cost would be exorbitant for just the fabric alone.

Jake had never seen him before, and no one was exactly rushing over to claim the body. The guy stared up at the ceiling, his mouth slack and his face registering surprise.

As he headed to the phone behind the bar to call the cops, he looked at the crowd of shocked faces among the patrons. A few people laughed as they stared at the mountain of flesh on the floor. He looked like the proverbial beached whale.

"All right. It's not funny, you assholes," he said. He could just imagine what would happen next, with the jokes that would start.

The cops came, along with the EMTs. They quickly verified the man was dead.

"We'll put him on a stretcher but this guy must weigh four hundred pounds. I don't know how we'll get him through the door of the Poodle—he's too wide," one of them explained to Jake and George.

The cops and EMTs rolled the man onto the stretcher and securely strapped the dead mountain of flesh to the sagging board. They tilted it on end, and jockeyed it out the door. It took several people to get the man and stretcher outside and into the ambulance.

Jake scratched his head. "How the hell did the man get in the door in the first place?"

AFTER THAT EXCITEMENT, the Poodle quickly settled down.

"George," Jake sighed, "give me another, and while you're at it, check out the bimbos, will ya? See if there's anything decent enough for me."

George pushed the drink in front of him. "Hey, I ain't your fuckin' pimp," and stalked away.

Jake needed to tell George he was only kidding. But on second thought, fuck him. And fuck the Poodle. He really had to get out of there.

The Orion Room still hadn't called back for a second interview. It had been well over two weeks, and Jake was getting antsy. Despite the recent larger paycheck that reflected his raise, he wanted to get the hell out of the Poodle.

Jake turned around and assumed his regular position of leaning on the bar, surveying the room, and enjoying a drink and a cigarette. Jake called George over. "Hey, why is this night different than all other nights?"

George replied, "What the fuck are you talking about?"

"It's one of the four questions they ask at Passover Dinner— why is this night different than all other nights?"

"So?"

Jake waved him away. "Forget it, George. Go wait on the customers."

Why did he happen to think of that? Bit of a non sequitor. But tonight *did* feel different.

He lit another cigarette. He couldn't identify the feeling he had that something bad was going to happen, and soon. Aside from the four-hundred-pound dead man, it had been relatively quiet for days. Something George always said came to mind. "The longer the calm, the bigger the storm."

"Yeah, right. George the philosopher," Jake muttered to himself and stubbed out his cigarette. He ordered another drink. His fifth? He'd lost count—he couldn't remember and he couldn't have cared less.

An hour later, Jake leaned on the bar, finished his sixth— or was it seventh?—bourbon and soda, and lit another cigarette. He thought about life—about managing the Poodle, about Kelly and the kids, about the possibility of a new job. Mostly, he thought about the cops' inability to nail Lucky Doyle for Dawn's murder.

He downed the last of his drink and set the empty glass on the bar. Tonight, the booze didn't alleviate the all-consuming hatred he felt for that sonofabitch, Doyle.

"I need to find a way to get this guy, and then let my inner Mr. Hyde come out," Jake muttered to no one in particular as he angrily stubbed out his cigarette. He reached into his pack for a fresh one.

The front door opened, followed immediately by a blast of cold air that hit Jake's back like an Arctic wind blowing over an igloo. Jake shivered.

"Where's Sherman?" growled a familiar voice.

Jake's head jerked up. Speaking of the devil. *Lucky Doyle.*

One of the customers shouted, "Doyle's got a gun! He's got a *gun!*"

Acting purely on instinct, as if he'd done it many times before, Jake reached for the .357 magnum holstered under his left arm.

He felt relaxed; the moment had finally arrived. This wasn't a dream.

He withdrew his gun. Gotcha!

Jake slowly turned and saw Doyle a few feet inside the door, coming toward him with a glazed look in his eyes. Jake's vision narrowed on Doyle, and everything else receded. Jake had played this scene several times in his mind and in his nightmares, and he knew exactly what to do.

Jake stared at him in contempt. "This one's for Dawn," Jake said quietly as he pulled the trigger.

The shot hit Lucky in the chest. The impact slammed Doyle up against the cigarette machine.

Jake walked slowly toward him, and said, "And these are for me." He emptied his gun into Doyle's chest. His body twitched and jerked, slumping to the floor and leaving a streak of blood down the front of the machine.

Jake stood over him, mesmerized, the gun still aimed at Doyle. "If I had more bullets, I'd still be firing into you, you sorry piece of shit."

His gun clicked. It was empty. His arm dropped to his side and he stared at the widening pool of blood. Doyle's eyes stared—sightlessly, but wide-eyed with horror—back at Jake.

Jake nudged him with his left foot, just to make sure. No response. *You're dead, you sonofabitch. You're dead.* His mind refused to move beyond that. Dead. Doyle was dead at last. He'd gotten him. He got Doyle before Doyle could get him, or Kelly, or another young woman. Dead. Doyle was dead.

He was vaguely aware of people shouting. Jake glanced up when two uniformed cops approached him—one of them was Frank MacPherson.

MacPherson held out his hand. "Give me the gun, Jake, and go sit down." He motioned toward an empty table a dozen feet away.

Jake did as he was told. From where he sat, he could see Doyle's body. Dead. Doyle was dead. A great sense of relief filled him.

Frank followed Jake to the table and said quietly, "Dummy up. Do *not* talk to anyone." He lit a cigarette and handed it to Jake.

When Jake took the cigarette from Frank, he was surprised at how steady his hands were. He was aware of what was going on around him, but it was as if it was a dream—another dream. He felt calm, but numb.

Jake watched Frank tell the other officer to move all the customers to the other side of the bar. He overheard MacPherson ask George, "What the hell happened?"

"I was in the can, taking a leak, when I heard the shots. Fuck! I've been afraid it would come to this."

MacPherson growled, "Do me a favor and don't fucking repeat to *anybody* what you just said to me."

George nodded and caught Jake's eye. In a haze, Jake watched him take the toothpick out, and mouth the words, "Man, you are really fucked."

Jake returned his gaze to Doyle's body. Two dead bodies in one night. But this one was a little more bloody than the earlier one. And they shouldn't have any trouble getting Doyle's body out the door.

Jake was vaguely aware of two detectives arriving a few minutes later. MacPherson had been kneeling over the body, his back to the room, but he stood up when the detectives entered the Poodle. One of them walked over to Doyle's body. "Jesus fuckin' Christ. Talk about overkill." He turned to MacPherson. "Where's the shooter?"

Frank pointed to Jake. The second detective said to MacPherson, "Thanks, Officer. We'll take it from here."

They read Jake his rights and cuffed him. On the way out the door, he passed Doyle's lifeless body.

He'd done what he'd intended to do: revenge Dawn's and the other girl's deaths, stop Doyle from coming after Kelly, and stop him from killing any more innocent women.

They led him outside, where two police cars were double parked, their lights flashing. A crowd had gathered, but Jake ignored them.

He ducked his head as he got into the backseat and slid over to the far side, away from the curious onlookers clogging the sidewalk.

Frank had followed them outside. He came over to the car and bent down to look in the window at Jake. The detectives tried to wave him away, but Frank called out, "You take care of yourself, Jake," through the closed window.

As the car pulled away from the curb, reality set in like a slap in the face.

What the fuck had he done?

He looked around, trying to see the cops through the metal grid between the front and back seats. His arms already ached from being twisted behind him and handcuffed.

"Hey, Ma. I'm not on top of the fuckin' world anymore," he whispered, his head bowed.

All too soon, the car pulled up in front of the Hennepin County Jail, located in the courthouse building and about a mile from the Poodle. There, they fingerprinted and photographed him.

As they took him to his cell, one of the guards whispered to him, "As far as I'm concerned, you performed a public service tonight."

He looked at the guard. That's easy for you to say, he thought.

They placed him in a cell by himself, thank God. He didn't think he could have survived being locked up with criminals. The door clanged closed behind him.

Alone, Jake began to shake. The alcohol was wearing off. The adrenaline rush had subsided, and he rocked back and forth. He was terrified of what would happen next. He called for the guard, but no one came. He rattled the door, but it was locked, of course.

Jake took a deep breath but that did no good. Instead, bile rose in his throat and he gulped it back down. He slammed his fist against the bars, and cried out, "How the *fuck* did I get into this mess?"

JAKE DIDN'T SLEEP. HE SPENT THE ENTIRE NIGHT berating himself for completely fucking up his life.

He paced the floor, and even banged his head against the wall a couple of times, but it hurt too much. And it didn't alleviate the hopelessness he felt. He held his head in his hands and tried to think what to do next, but he had no answers. All he had were questions. What was going to happen to him? How would Kelly react when she saw this in the newspaper, on television, or when people were talking about it? What would his kids think of him?

He hugged himself and rocked back and forth again. He had a sudden urge to puke. As he wiped the vomit from his mouth on his sleeve, he noticed blood on his shirt. Doyle's blood. *Damn that man! It's his fault I'm here!*

But at least the scumbag will never kill again, he tried to console himself. Then he tried praying to God that if, by some miracle, he got out of this mess, he would change. He would get his shit together and—

Who was he kidding? He was a mess. His fuckin' life was over. He just got done murdering someone, he was hung over, he was in jail . . . and he was more scared than he'd ever been in his life.

And then he puked again.

CHAPTER 23

Friday, December 7

THE CELL DOOR OPENED. JAKE JUMPED; he hadn't heard the guards approaching. There were two of them. An older man, fat, maybe fiftyish and a younger man, well-built and looking very proper.

Jake felt sick. He had a hard time just standing up.

The older guard spoke. "Time to go. You're due to appear in court. Jesus Christ, you look like you've been on a bender for a week."

The younger one muttered something Jake couldn't quite hear, but he did catch the word, "disgusting."

They cuffed him, but this time in front, and as they walked down the hall, Jake asked the heavyset guard, "What time is it?"

The fat man said, "It's almost ten o'clock." They stopped partway down a corridor. "I'm going to take you to the bathroom, so you can clean yourself up."

The other one, who didn't seem to like the idea of stopping, said that they would be right outside the door, "So don't try any funny business."

They took his cuffs off. The younger guard opened a plastic bag he'd been carrying and gave him back his belt, tie, shoes, and sport coat.

Jake walked into the bathroom, grateful it was empty. He looked into the mirror. Staring back at him was a stranger: unshaven, with deep bags under his bloodshot eyes. His hair was matted, his skin was gray-tinged, and his eyes looked vacant. "Who is this guy?" he thought—or yelled. He wasn't sure which.

He felt himself losing it as he gripped the sink. "I'm probably going away for the rest of my life." He wasn't sure if that was worse than a death sentence, but this was Minnesota, so that option wasn't on the menu.

As he leaned over the sink, the dry heaves shook his body. Thankfully, his body soon stopped convulsing. He took a deep breath and proceeded to wash up as best he could. The sport coat and tie covered the puke stains on his shirt but not on his trousers. The smell was overwhelming.

He left the bathroom and the guards put the cuffs back on him. They joined several other handcuffed prisoners and their guards. He purposely didn't make eye contact with any of the others. Even in the present company, he felt embarrassed and alone.

The group entered what looked like a freight elevator. Jake's heavyset guard pushed the button for the second floor and the car descended slowly. Jake and his fellow prisoners were brought into a courtroom through a rear entrance.

He was surprised to see his buddy Neal Phillips—aka the Judge—standing in the gallery. Neal gave him the high sign. George was also there, in the back row, without his toothpick. Jake caught a quick glance of a tall guy with wiry dark hair standing next to George. It looked like Buddy Goldberg, a bail bondsman Jake had a nodding acquaintance with.

Jake almost sagged in relief. Now at least he wasn't alone.

He felt like shit and he knew he looked it. In addition to the vomit stains, his clothes were rumpled. Jake battled a hangover, and his mouth tasted like an ashtray. He desperately needed a cigarette, a cup of coffee—and a drink.

The guards led the prisoners to the jury box and motioned for them to sit down. Jake turned and looked at the other pathetic-looking losers and wondered if they felt as helpless as he did.

The bailiff entered and intoned, "Please rise. The Honorable Judge David Osborne is presiding."

An older man in a black robe entered from the judge's chambers. He didn't make eye contact with any prisoners, although Jake watched him closely, knowing his fate—his immediate fate, anyway—was in this man's hands.

Jake's brain was racing. He felt sick again. He was tired, depressed, and still couldn't think clearly. After the judge sat down, so did everyone else, including Jake.

The bailiff spoke again. "Case #93742. The State of Minnesota vs. Jacob Sherman." He motioned for Jake to come forward and stand before the judge's bench.

"Mr. Sherman, you stand before the court, charged with second-degree murder." The judge looked down at Jake.

Jake swallowed and, not for the first time, realized the enormity of the situation. Murder! His first instinct was to run, but his feet didn't move.

Impatiently, the judge asked, "What do you want to do today? Do you have an attorney?"

"Your Honor," Neal Phillips called from the back of the room. Jake turned and watched Neal approach the bench. "Neal Phillips will represent the defendant in this matter."

The black-robed judge nodded. "And for the people?" He looked over at the prosecutor's table, and Jake followed his gaze.

A man in a dark suit and tie, with a crisp white shirt, stood up. He was about the same age as Jake. "Your Honor, Alan Ginsburg, Assistant Hennepin County Attorney on behalf of the state. The charge is murder, and we request he be remanded with no bail, as we are considering a more serious charge."

What could possibly be more serious than murder? Jake muttered to himself.

The judge looked at Jake over the top of his glasses, and then at Neal. "Mr. Phillips? What do you have to say?"

"Your Honor, Mr. Ginsburg has forgotten that every defendant in this state is entitled to bail. That said, Mr. Sherman is a member in good standing in this community. He has no criminal record, he's not about to flee, nor is he—"

Ginsburg leaped to his feet. "Your Honor, the defendant shot the victim six times—"

The judge held up his hand in Ginsburg's direction. "I've heard enough. Save your arguments for trial. The bail is set at $15,000, cash or bond." He thumped his gavel on his desk. "Next case."

Neal leaned over and whispered in Jake's ear, "Buddy Goldberg is posting your bail as we speak, you lucky sonofabitch."

"Who . . . ?" Jake asked. Who had paid for his bond?

"Hey, don't look a gift horse in the mouth, schmuck," Neal fired back.

Jake teared up and grabbed Neal's hand. He gave it a big squeeze. "Thanks, man. Thanks." He'd figure it out later and thank that person.

For the first time since Doyle walked into the bar last night, Jake felt like he could breathe. He would get outta there for now, at least. Thank God. Now he'd get that cigarette, cup of coffee—and a drink.

"They're going to take you back to your cell now, Jake, and you'll probably be released before the end of the day." Neal put his arm around Jake for a moment. "Be sure to call me later."

TWO HOURS LATER, A GUARD CAME to Jake's cell to tell him the paperwork for his bond had been processed so he was being released.

George waited for him just outside the last locked door. Jake collected his watch and wallet from the property room and signed all the necessary paperwork. He knew he'd had some cash in his wallet but didn't bother to check if it was still there; he just wanted to get the hell outside.

As he walked through the door, George slapped Jake on the back. "You look like shit, you crazy son of a bitch! And as I always suspected, your balls are bigger than your brains."

Jake, still in a daze, grew lightheaded as he breathed deeply of the fresh air. "Please, take me somewhere that I can get coffee and some food. I'm dying here." His stomach was growling relentlessly and he had a headache from the hangover and hunger. "Take me to some greasy spoon."

George took him to Denny's for breakfast. "You look like one of my dogs just before I put him down," George commented with a sideways glance at Jake as they entered the restaurant.

Jake ignored him and headed straight to the cigarette machine, where he purchased a pack of Winstons and lit one up. He took a long drag on the cigarette and let it out slowly. It was comforting, and his hands finally quit shaking.

He slid into the booth where George was already ordering a pot of coffee. Jake placed his order for his usual big breakfast. George didn't order anything for himself beyond coffee.

With the first bite of his eggs, Jake gagged. His stomach balked. "I think I'm going to puke."

George immediately leaned back. "If you puke on me, you won't have to worry about your future, because I'll end it for you right now," he said with a grin.

Jake tried a bite of plain toast and decided he wasn't going to throw up after all. After a few more bites, he asked the question that had been forefront in his mind for the past few hours.

"Who the hell put up the bail for me?" Jake asked.

George explained that Pat had called Neal Phillips earlier that morning, and he also called Buddy Goldberg, so they could be there for Jake's court appearance.

"So who the hell put up my bail?"

"Pat and I agreed to split it, so don't go skipping out on me," he said, only half kidding. "Pat has contacted Ron Meshbesher about defending you," he continued. "You really don't want Neal, because this is way over his fuckin' head. Apparently, Meshbesher owes Pat and the Old Man a favor. Meshbesher wouldn't make any promises, but he at least agreed to talk. Be sure and call him as soon as you get home."

Shit. That wasn't any help, not when he couldn't afford to pay the guy. Meshbesher was the number one defense attorney in Minneapolis, if not the entire Midwest. After all, Meshbesher was the one who helped Jimmy Box beat the murder rap.

Jake didn't bother to hide his sarcasm. "That's just great," he said. "I happen to know that he gets up to twenty-five grand for murder cases. I don't have more than a few hundred bucks!"

George snarled, "Don't be so fucking negative. Besides, don't call it *murder*; it was *self defense*," he said with a big grin that carried no mirth.

Jake's headache felt like someone had run over his head, and now that he'd had some food, he just wanted to go home and sleep. "George, please take me to my car. Let's get the hell out of here." George nodded and they both stood up. "Oh, and incidentally, do I still have a job?"

George looked at him like he was crazy. "Pat said to take a few days off and then call him."

That probably meant he didn't have a job. Fuck.

The bile rose in his throat again. He went outside for fresh air and another cigarette, leaving George behind to pick up the bill.

Neither man spoke on the way to the parking lot near the Poodle where Jake's car was still parked. As he got out of George's car, Jake said, "I don't know how to thank you for what you've done, George. I owe you *big* time."

George held up his hand as if to fend off any additional words of thanks. "Don't go getting mushy. You would've done the same for me."

Jake found the parking lot attendant and paid. Two days' worth of parking took all his spare cash he discovered was still in his wallet.

As he sat in his car while it warmed up, it started to snow. He reminded himself to be extra careful as he drove home and not to break any speeding laws. That's all he needed right now, a speeding ticket.

His thoughts turned to what he would say to Kelly. She would be his first call as soon as he got home. Even before he called Meshbesher.

ACTUALLY, THE FIRST THING HE DID when he got home was to peel off his clothes and get into the shower. He turned on the water full blast and just stood there, face up, letting the water strike him hard for at least ten minutes.

He finally summoned the energy to lather up. He scrubbed

hard but didn't feel clean. It was as if he was trying to wash away the killing, the arrest, and his night in jail, but with no success.

His life would never be the same—that is, if he were to ever *have* a life. He felt embarrassed and full of self-loathing. What a dumb, dumb sonofabitch he was. Everything was really fucked up. Whose fault was this, anyway? Who got the blame?

He got out of the shower and looked in the mirror.

"Guess what, asshole?" he said to his reflection. "*You're* to blame."

He dreaded making the call to Kelly, but he wanted to get to her before she heard about his release on TV. She would be pissed off that it had taken him so long to call her. But that was the least of it. He didn't even know if she would talk to him.

With a towel wrapped around him, he went into the kitchen, reached into the cupboard, and pulled out a bottle of Jim Beam. He poured a half glass and took a big gulp, hoping it would give him enough courage. He wasn't used to drinking it straight, without any soda, so it burned his throat on the way down. He shivered.

The second swallow didn't burn as much.

He reached reluctantly for the phone. I've just got to suck it up and do this, he thought.

He called the furniture store where Kelly worked and asked for her. The man that answered didn't even ask who was calling. He could hear people talking excitedly in the background and could only imagine what they were saying.

Kelly came to the phone and, without asking who it was, practically shouted, "Jake, why did it take you so long to call me?" She didn't wait for an answer. "Do you have any idea how much I worried?"

Jake didn't know what to say. He had expected something different. He thought there would be recriminations but to his surprise, there were none.

"Jake, are you still there?"

He swallowed hard. "I couldn't call until now. I was released this morning, made bail, and drove home to clean up. Also, I, I didn't know what to say to you." His voiced cracked and he started to cry, "I'm, I'm so ashamed and—" He completely lost it, and sobbed uncontrollably, the phone still up to his ear.

Kelly remained silent. After a few moments, she cleared her throat and said, "Jake, you must get a hold of yourself and start thinking. You'll need to find a good lawyer, and I don't mean Neal Phillips. Now, I really have to get back to work, but call me tonight. Do you promise?"

"Okay . . . I, I promise," he got out in between sobs and hung up the phone.

JAKE SPENT THE NEXT FEW MINUTES beating himself up some more and, after exhausting all the self-insults he could think of and chain-smoking nearly half a pack of cigarettes, he finished his drink and pulled himself together. He looked up Ron Meshbesher's phone number and placed the call.

Ron took his call right away and after a few pleasantries, they got down to business. Ron asked what questions the police had asked and what he had told them.

"That was the crazy part," Jake replied. "They didn't ask me anything regarding the shooting, and I didn't tell them anything."

"Okay, that's good. I don't want you to discuss this problem with anyone, and I mean *anyone!*" Meshbesher said.

"Does that mean you will represent me?" Jake asked hopefully.

"I'm not sure and I can't make you any promises, but why don't you come to my office today at four-thirty and we'll discuss this further?"

Jake agreed and hung up the phone, pleased Meshbesher would see him. Then a thought occurred to him. Was Meshbesher just seeing him to pacify the Blumenthals because he owed them a favor? Jake's shoulders slumped.

He needed another drink, but instead, he decided to go for a walk. Maybe the fresh air would be good for his headache, and he wanted to stay sober for his meeting with Meshbesher.

It was a typical Minnesota day in December. The temperature had to be below zero, it was snowing, and the winds were picking up. He bundled up as best he could. Not being the outdoors type, he didn't have the appropriate clothing. Nevertheless, he went out, determined to walk a couple of miles.

As he wandered mindlessly through his neighborhood, he stared at the ground in front of him, reliving the events of last night. He tried to analyze his feelings about killing Doyle because he hadn't really let himself think about it yet today, especially since his release.

He kept running the scene at the Poodle through his mind but didn't have any answers. He was numb and still in shock, he figured. He still felt relieved that Doyle wouldn't hurt anyone else, but in terms of his own role in stopping Doyle . . . well, his mind went blank and shut down.

A couple blocks later, a thought popped into his head, something his friend, artist Marshall Ferster, had written to him on a painting some time ago. "To my good friend Jake. What good does it do you to be right?"

He gave up walking after twenty minutes of freezing his ass off. Surprisingly, it had helped to clear his head.

He went back to the house, set his alarm for three-thirty, and crashed.

CHAPTER 24

Friday, December 7

JAKE LEFT MESHBESHER'S OFFICE with, for the first time, hope. What he and Meshbesher had talked about might save Jake's bacon in the long run. By the end of the meeting, Meshbesher had been cautiously optimistic.

Meshbesher had asked very little about the actual shooting, but he was inordinately curious about the connection between the Poodle and the Hotel Anthony.

"Why are you asking me so much about the Poodle and the Anthony?"

"If I'm going to help you beat this rap, I need something—anything—and I've heard some tales about what goes on at the Anthony. Is there anything there that you can tell me, that we can use as leverage with the County Attorney?"

"Leverage? You mean . . . blackmail?" Jake asked, stunned.

Meshbesher looked bemused. "That's a poor choice of words, Jake."

Meshbesher was right. "Leverage" was a better word, and if it was leverage he wanted, that's what Jake would give him. He thought long and hard. "Well, I know there's gambling, and lots of hookers. I know there are some upstanding members of the community going in and out—"

"Who?" Meshbesher demanded. Jake told him the names he'd drug out of Reggie.

"Hmm. *Very* interesting." Meshbesher all but rubbed his hands together in glee. He narrowed his gaze at Jake and said expectantly, "What else you got?"

Shit. Jake tensed, frustrated that he couldn't come up with anything else. Meshbesher obviously expected more.

There must be something else he knew . . . Then an idea came to mind. "I don't know what you're looking for, exactly, but are you familiar with the Freddie Gates robbery?"

"I recall it, but how is that relevant?" Meshbesher looked skeptical.

"Well, as you know, Freddie Gates was Humphrey's right hand man, so he had access to pretty much everything Humphrey did. Gates died and his funeral was attended by several well-known dignitaries, including Humphrey. Gates' grandchildren were young teenagers at the time, and they stayed at Gates' house during the funeral. Three guys entered the house, tied up the children—but didn't hurt them—and broke into the safe. As far as the public and press were concerned, only money and assorted valuables were taken."

Meshbesher raised his eyebrows. "So far you haven't said anything I don't know. There must be more to the story. What is it?"

Jake paused as he decided to tell Meshbesher only part of what he knew, at least for now. It wasn't so much that he wasn't sure if he could trust the attorney, but his instincts told him not to say too much at this juncture.

Meshbesher motioned impatiently for him to continue.

"Okay, so, what I learned was that two hundred and fifty thousand dollars and some papers were taken."

"Hold it! A quarter of a million? And what kind of papers?" Meshbesher sat up straight and stopped toying with the pen he'd been twirling lazily while Jake talked.

Jake continued, pleased he had Ron's attention. "That's the interesting part. Through an intermediary, Humphrey's people requested that if the papers were returned, the money could be kept and they would consider the matter closed." Jake leaned forward and looked Meshbesher in the eye. "You can come to your own conclusion as to what was in those papers."

Ron pinched the bridge of his nose and stared at Jake. "That's quite a story. Who is your source?"

Jake replied, "I can't tell you that. But what I can tell you, is this." He leaned across the desk and whispered a few details into Meshbesher's ear. Ron's eyes widened and Jake leaned back in his seat. "If I told you more, I'd have to kill you."

Meshbesher laughed uncomfortably.

Jake still hadn't told him that he knew who the people were that had committed the robbery, and that he had a good idea who had set the whole thing up. But he wasn't about to reveal those details to Meshbesher because he didn't want to get the Judge in trouble.

Meshbesher nodded. "Okay, okay. I guess I don't need to know your source, for now. Hell, what you've told me should be plenty. So, I want you to go home, Jake. And let me reiterate that you should not discuss anything that was said here, or anything about the case—whatsoever—with anyone."

"Will do," Jake agreed. "What's the next step?"

"I'll think about what we discussed, and I'll get back to you when I decide what to do with this information—how I'm going to *leverage* it," Ron said.

"Does this mean you're taking my case? And if so, what kind of a fee are we talking about?"

Ron nodded. "This is so juicy," he laughed, "that I'm going to do this for you *pro bono* . . . and me, a lifelong Democrat, just like Gates and Humphrey. I'm almost ashamed of myself," he guffawed.

Relief flooded Jake. Thrilled, he shook Ron's hand vigorously. When he left the building a few moments later, he turned up his collar against the bitter cold as he walked briskly to the lot where he'd parked his Mustang.

After clearing the snow off of the windshield, Jake got in, warmed up the car, and hesitated before leaving the lot. He thought about going to a bar to celebrate Meshbesher taking his case pro bono. No, he decided, and headed directly for home.

He vowed, "I promise you, God, that there'll be no more trouble from The Jake." And he firmly believed it.

JAKE SAT AT HIS KITCHEN COUNTER, lit another cigarette, and took a big swig of his Beam and soda. He looked at the calendar on the wall. It had been exactly six days since the shooting.

He'd talked to Meshbesher a couple of times, and things were progressing well on that front.

But Jake had nothing but time on his hands and, not surprisingly, he kept thinking about Doyle's death. He couldn't stop reliving the incident, over and over. Beyond the obvious—that he'd killed a man—something nagged at him about that night, but he couldn't put his finger on it. When the image of Doyle's dead body came to mind for the umpteenth time, he finally admitted to himself that he had absolutely no remorse for killing Doyle.

So what kind of person did that make him?

Someone very much like Mr. Hyde, he answered himself.

On the other hand, Lucky was a piece of shit who had most likely killed at least two young women. The bastard had sliced them with some kind of knife—

He suddenly realized what was bothering him about the night of the shooting. Lucky didn't have a gun!

Are you sure? Are you sure? He pounded his forehead. It couldn't be, and yet now it was crystal clear to Jake. The son of a bitch hadn't been carrying, Jake was sure of it. Yet the police had found a gun on him, so how . . . ?

Aha! Somebody planted it. It must've been George. "Oh man!" he said out loud, "do I ever owe him." George hadn't said anything and Jake didn't plan on mentioning it to him. The less said, the better. What a pal George was. He didn't know another person who would've stuck his neck out like that. Jake only hoped that someday he could return the favor.

Jake looked down at the ashtray overflowing with butts. The place reeked of smoke. He poured himself another drink and lit another cigarette.

Meshbesher was due to meet with the County Attorney on the twenty-fourth, and there wasn't anything Jake could do but wait out the next twelve days. He had called Blumenthal to see if he could come back to work. Pat seemed pretty evasive about when that would be. Jake took that as confirmation that he didn't have a job anymore.

Just great, he thought, and with Christmas just around the corner. No money coming in. How was he going to provide any semblance of a normal Christmas for the kids if he didn't have any money for presents?

JAKE STIRRED AND THRASHED ABOUT in his bed. Some god-awful noise made him sit up with a start. The damned telephone was ringing.

He ran to the kitchen to answer it. "What?" he shouted into the receiver and glanced at the clock. It was four in the morning.

"Jake!" his younger sister, Judy, said. "The Poodle and the Hotel Anthony are burning! They say it will be a complete loss."

Jake was stunned into silence.

His sister asked, "Jake, are you still there?"

Wide awake now, he asked, "Was anybody killed? Do you have any details?"

"All they're saying on the radio is that it's a five-alarm fire and they think everyone got out."

He thought about it for a minute. No one was hurt, so beyond that, it was no sweat off his balls.

"Well," he told her, "that's too bad, but I no longer have a job there, so frankly, my dear, I don't give a shit. By the way, what the hell are you doing up at four in the morning? On second thought, I don't want to know."

Jake hung up and knew he couldn't go back to sleep. He thought about the fire and the devastation it had caused, and decided he really did give a shit. After all, the Poodle—for better or worse— had been a big part of his life for a year. And Pat and George had posted his bail.

He made some coffee, lit up another Winston, and turned on the radio. The fire was a major story.

The announcer said, "A five-alarm fire earlier today destroyed the main portion of the Hotel Anthony and Poodle Bar & Restaurant at 806 Hennepin Avenue. There were no deaths reported, but fire officials said they couldn't be sure until the rubble is searched. Several dozen people were rescued from fire escapes while others got out before the fire had begun to spread. Also in the news—"

Jake turned off the radio and stared up at the ceiling. He wasn't surprised that something like this would have happened, and he wondered whose handiwork it was. He couldn't go back to the Poodle now even if he wanted to. Even if they wanted him back. The Poodle—the home away from home for so many people—was no more.

THE TWENTY-FOURTH OF DECEMBER finally rolled around. He hadn't shaved in a few days and the kitchen sink overflowed with dirty dishes. He'd found he enjoyed long walks in the bitter cold. He tried to stay somewhat sober, but it always ended up the same— with a shrug and a muttered, "What the fuck," followed by him pouring himself a drink.

Nobody had called. Not his friends, not his family. It was almost like he didn't exist anymore. If self-pity was money, I'd be a millionaire, he thought as he hunched his shoulders against the biting wind during his morning walk. He turned the corner and saw his house ahead. He checked his watch. Time to head back to the house and wait for Meshbesher's phone call.

When he got inside the warm house and removed his outerwear, he paced. After several minutes, he'd had enough. He couldn't wait for Meshbesher to call him, so he picked up the phone and dialed the man's downtown office.

Jake had to leave a message, but Meshbesher returned his call quickly.

"Jake, I understand they call you *The Jake*, so from now on, you can call me Mr. Perry Fuckin' Mason!"

Meshbesher sounded jubilant. Jake's heart skipped a beat. "Tell me, tell me."

"Well, Jake, my boy, do you want the good news or the bad news?"

"Hey, Ron, don't mess with me. I'm about ready to have a heart attack."

"Okay, okay. The good news is that they're not going to charge you. And you're free. Or almost free. The bad news—and this is the deal I made—is that you have to leave town for the foreseeable future."

Jake was elated and stunned. He collapsed into the nearest chair. "Well, when do I have to go?"

"The sooner, the better," Meshebesher stated slowly and emphatically.

"Well, what the hell does that mean?" Jake grunted. How soon is soon? And what about Kelly and the kids? How was he going to tell them?

"Tomorrow wouldn't be too soon," Meshbesher replied.

Jake sighed and knew he'd been let off more than easy. The nightmare was over. And he owed it all to Meshebesher. "I can't tell you enough how much this means to me. I kinda owe you my life, Ron."

"You know, I never told you why I really took this case. Between you and me, I wanted to stick it to the County Attorney's office due to another situation, so let's call it even. Good luck to ya, Jake."

They said good-bye and Jake hung up the receiver, his head spinning. He was free! But God, he had to leave town tomorrow? Were they crazy?

On the other hand, he didn't want them to change their fuckin' mind. Fine. He'd leave town. It was a helluva lot better than going to jail.

He needed to think this thing through, and quickly. Where would he go? What would he do? He didn't have much money and his car needed new brakes at the very least. Mexico popped into his head. What if he drove down there and got lost? No one would even know or care. Everything seemed hopeless. He had no job, no money, and no family.

Maybe he should just end it all.

He contemplated the various methods he could use. A gun—but he didn't have his gun anymore. He could stick his head in a gas oven, but his was electric. He could stab himself, but success wasn't guaranteed. He could hang himself, but he didn't have any rope.

Lighting up another cigarette, he pondered other methods to end this despair. He could use poison, but he sure as hell didn't have any of that sitting around the house. Or, he sighed, I could run in front of a speeding car . . . but dammit, it's winter and there's snow on the ground, and nobody's fucking speeding.

He suddenly came up short. What would his suicide do to his children? He had known a guy in high school whose father had killed himself, and the kid was scarred for life. Okay, that option was eliminated. He didn't want to cause his kids more grief than he already had.

So going down to Mexico was his best choice. He planned his route and remembered he had an old friend who lived in Denver. If he could stop there, halfway to Mexico, he could spend the night and be across the border after two or three long days of driving.

He placed the call to Denver and his friend, Jack, answered. "Come stay as long as you like, Jake. We have plenty of room."

Finally, a yes. After all the bad crap and the indifference, someone wanted him.

Jake decided to tell the children and Kelly in person. The thought of doing so was almost as agonizing as the possibility of going to prison had been. His stomach cramped and tightened, so he set those thoughts aside and focused on what else he needed to do to leave. Calling his mother and sisters to say good-bye was about it.

Jake grimaced and wished he could just sneak out of town and avoid the good-byes altogether. They hurt too much.

He called Kelly, who answered on the second ring.

"They're not going to press charges," he said with no fanfare.

"That's great, Jake, but what does that mean?" she asked.

"Basically, it means I'm free."

"Oh, Jake, I'm really happy for you," she cried.

"I'd like to come over before you and the kids go to your mom's for Christmas Eve, because I have something else I need to tell you."

She sighed. "Okay. Come about four."

He hung up and tried to avoid thinking about meeting with them. Instead, he occupied himself once again with preparing to leave. He really had nothing to take with him except some clothes and a few personal items. Some pictures of Kelly and the kids. He'd travel light—whatever could fit in the Mustang.

He called his mother and two sisters to let them know he'd be leaving town for a while. They were surprised and happy to hear he wasn't going to jail. His mother told him to take care of himself, and that was about all she said. She's not a warm, fuzzy person, my mother, Jake thought with a twinge of sadness.

After all those calls, Jake was tired of talking. He just wanted to disappear, but he still had the conversation with Kelly and the kids to get through. It crossed his mind to call George and maybe Pat, but he thought, Nah, I'm emotionally spent, and I gotta save whatever I got left for Kelly and the kids.

He packed up his car with everything but his shaving kit and one change of clothes he'd need in the morning. He checked his watch. Three o'clock. He muttered, "Well, I guess it's time."

During the forty-five-minute drive to Kelly's, he tried to figure out what he was going to say. After several conversations with himself, he decided the best approach was a positive one.

He arrived at Kelly's house and pulled up in the back, through the alley, where he usually parked. Kelly answered as soon as he knocked.

"I want to talk to you first," he said when she opened the door. She nodded silently.

He followed her into the living room because the kids were upstairs getting ready. She looked festive and gorgeous in a long, black velvet skirt and white blouse. Her heels clicked on the hardwood floor. He felt terribly sad as he watched her walk ahead of him. This felt so final.

She turned and faced him with a worried look. "Okay, what's up?"

He told her the details of his conversation with Meshbesher, although it was hard to get the words out. When he got to the part about him needing to leave town, her jaw dropped and her eyes welled up with tears.

Jake was also on the verge of tears. He put his arms around her and hugged her tightly. Kelly cried on his shoulder for a few moments and then gently disengaged herself from him.

She let out a big sigh and wiped away her lingering tears. "Maybe it's for the best, Jake. Now pull yourself together and let's go up and talk to the children."

Jake cleared his throat and slowly walked up the stairs. This time, Kelly followed him. He took a deep, deep breath and said to himself, Okay, okay, think positive. Act positive.

The four of them sat on his daughter's bed while Jake explained, "I'm going to leave town for a while. But I want you to know that I'll write and call you often, and I love you both very much."

Sean and Sarah both cried. "Why?" They bombarded him with more questions. "For how long?" "Where are you going?" "Can we come see you?" Sean launched himself into Jake's lap, and Sara crawled across the bed to cling to him.

He hugged them both, and Kelly wrapped her arms around all three of them.

He could barely talk around the lump in his throat. "I'll let you know when I get settled, and we'll take it from there. I want you to behave yourselves, and listen to your mother."

As much as he hated to part with them, he couldn't wait to leave because he just couldn't take it anymore. The emotion was overwhelming. He hugged them again and squeezed real hard, then helped dry their tears.

He and Kelly headed back downstairs, where he said good-bye to her. He hugged her and kissed her one last time. By now, the lump in his throat was too big and he couldn't say a word.

"Take care of yourself, Jake. And you'd better tell us where you end up," she whispered.

His vision blurred as he took one last look at her and headed out the door.

On his drive back to Wayzata, he decided he was *not* going to go to a bar because he wanted to get up early and leave by six a.m. When he got home, he'd drink some water or a soda pop to help his dry mouth and the headache that pounded behind his sore, watery eyes.

CHAPTER 25

Tuesday, December 25

JAKE WOKE UP AT FIVE A.M. He had slept surprisingly well and felt pretty good.

He'd told his roommate last night that he was leaving. Since he was already paid up through the end of the month, there was no issue with the rent.

He went through his mental checklist to see if he had forgotten to pack something, but came up with nothing. He'd told Pete to keep anything he wanted and to shitcan the rest.

He backed out of the driveway and in a few minutes was on the highway going south out of town. He lit up a cigarette and lovingly patted the steering wheel. "Don't fail me now, baby," he urged the Mustang.

He changed lanes and exited onto the interstate that would take him in a southwesterly direction.

He settled back with his cigarette. Plenty of time to think. He started in with the usual self-recriminations: Losing his wife, losing his job, getting arrested for the murder of Lucky Doyle and, in general, making a mess of his life.

The future loomed before him—a giant question mark and as empty as the road he traveled. The words of comedian Lenny Bruce popped into his head. "You take your baggage with you." In other words, changing locations will provide the same results, unless *you* change.

Okay, he thought. Where did he start, because it was a long list.

Number one: He never wanted to see another gun.

Number two: He definitely had to cut down on his drinking.

Number three: He'd have to be willing to take some menial job where no references were required.

Number four: He had to let Kelly go, and give up on the dream of them being together again.

And number five: No more Mr. Hyde. He had to control his anger and that propensity toward violence that working at the Poodle had brought out in him.

He looked heavenward. *I promise, I promise. No more Mr. Hyde. Just the good Dr. Jekyll from here on out.*

Jake glanced at the speedometer. He was going sixty and couldn't push the Mustang for much more, despite the sparseness of traffic.

He thought about what lie at the end of the road. What the fuck did he think he was going to do in Mexico? He probably couldn't get a job down there, legally. What did they do there? Pick cotton? Grapes? Did they farm? Shit if he knew.

The rising sun distracted him. The pale blue sky didn't have a cloud in sight. The world was bathed in the soft hues of the sunrise, and everything looked fresh and clean. Full of promise.

Suddenly, he felt a surge of hope and optimism, although logically, he couldn't understand why.

But maybe he didn't have to.

He lit up a new cigarette and settled in for the long drive, remembering the famous quote from *Gone with the Wind*. A small smile stole over his face. He said to himself, "After all, Jake, tomorrow is another day."

MARVIN L. MILLER, spent 35 years in the hospitality industry in the Midwest and the West Coast. He ran restaurants and hotels with up to 400 people reporting to him. Therefore, he is very familiar with the situations that form the basis of this story. A keen observer of people coupled with his sharpened insight gives this book a realistic portrayal. During his career, Miller saw the best and worst of the human condition. These experiences led to his ability to accurately portray the unusual and memorable characters in *Jake's Dilemma*.